Other books by Sherrie DeMorrow:

Knight and Daye
Cloud of Dreams
The Elder Rose
All The Land
The Little Bird
Beyond the Land
A Little Princess
Romancing the West
The Silver Millions
The Painted Chapel
A Hound's Desire
Space of Things

SPACE OF THINGS

BY

SHERRIE DEMORROW

Published 2020 by

Lightning Source (UK) Ltd
Chapter House,
Pitfield,
Kiln Farm,
Milton Keynes
MK11 3LW,
UK

Cover Art Design by Sam Wall

To LL for help and support

In acknowledgment of PF, KA

and

To the memories of CR, LB, LLG, RL, and TO'C,
who inspired this story

PREFACE

Although this could not be mentioned before, please be advised that there are sections of this book, as in the previous books, that contain *actual* **life experiences, emotions and memories. In the guise of fiction, it is the only way to inform the public of the results of an extreme lifestyle and treatment toward a helpless child (now fully grown and** *still suffering daily, the aftershocks of such treatment***). It is to be further noted that this individual suffers from a spectrum disorder called Asperger's Syndrome, which is a form of Autism. The author hopes this will not affect the enjoyment of the following, as well as the previous stories already written.**

Despite the disclaimer in the aforementioned paragraph, please note this is still a book of fiction. The reader must suspend all preconceptions of belief in past history, as this book is not meant as an accurate representation of historical events (except in the case described in previous paragraph).

The historical attitudes towards sensitive issues, and people's prejudices of the time, had to remain intact to provide a sense of realism in the story. No historical figures represented herein had been harmed during the writing of this work. Any personalities referred to herein are used in loving tribute to them.

Some place names given are **NOT** real, unless otherwise stated or recognised as real (or based on real places). Other characters (for the most part) are fictional and loosely based on people known of by the author.

PROLOGUE

It was mid-morning on the planet Novaterra. The President of this newly-formed world of surviving humanity, was due to make a bid for negotiation to end the conflict with the aliens. Technology had taken a back seat; no one was progressing anymore, and it seemed that things were heading backward. It was the time of the Great Galactic Rubbish Recycling War and everyone was fighting for their lives.

Fierce battles waged on, and had done so for nearly a millennia. God knows why. The aliens being fought against showed no disposition toward a resolution, since the War's beginning. It was started when a former Earth woman named Cynthia Lear had sided herself with Spazio, the Valastron. She had an enormous grudge against humanity that was shared by the alien races allied to the Valastrons. Earth was invaded, depleted, and its inhabitants scattered. One of the planets they decided to settle on became Novaterra. It sustained life and colonisation. It also allowed them to continue the fight from a better distance. The Earth was too far away and became impossible to live on.

The President was poster-boy cute, sophisticated, highly intelligent, fully-human and brave. He was also under 50, a young man (in some circles) to sport such bravery in times like these. His charms had led him into much political satire that knew no bounds. Freedom of Speech was highly prized; no one cared what anyone said anymore. Yet by now, the War became a joke, due to its duration and inconsistent intents of the aliens. There was always someone there who wanted a fight, and they got one. It was a dire situation that everyone was drawn into, much like any cartoon of the 20th century.

The upcoming meeting could end this, and the President believed he could charm his way into a different kind of alien battlefield. Hey, if he can charm women, than the aliens should be easy!

He would match wits with them, testing the advanced behaviours of the many races that included humanoid, blob, and bug groups. It proved a worthy challenge, and if he did succeed, he would be remembered and cherished by all.

The motorcade proceeded through a highway, past an industrial centre that served during the War. They were the various recycling and manufacturing plants which worked on refurbishing old rubbish into fine weapons. Other buildings included a tower-block dorm for the workers, a commissary, and a library, full of ancient media artefacts of old, like printed books, compact discs and even old gramophone records that taught old languages and occasionally played music. Video game consoles also decorated the illustrious setting. Only the most nerd-minded paid such devotion to this history.

It wasn't long now before a turn came, right or left. The driver considered his options carefully, so as not to go to the wrong building. Unfortunately, they looked the same, due to budget constraints, so they were left with edificial distinctions that held no imagination. The navigation system in the car went dead for some reason. The driver banged on the dashboard, and the lights flashed for a moment... then dimmed softly to nil.

'Dammit! Why couldn't they get a new nav system? I thought this was fixed,' he cried aloud.

'Don't worry,' an advisor recommended, 'I know where this place is. Turn left on Beagle Avenue.'

The left turn was made, as more solemn buildings loomed larger than the statues of Easter Island. Onc of them housed a pill depository, for those unable to cope with the present day experience.

There were many buildings like this, as the public suffered eating disorders and depression, because of scarcity of goals and toilet paper. These lean times could challenge even the most hearty anorexic.

In one of the depositories hid an unknown gunman, one that had guts, determination and alien DNA. He was ordered to stop the negotiations and carry on the War. He lay there, waiting for that cavalcade to shoot up his lane, as a needle to an eager drug addict.

Meanwhile, in the back of the President's vehicle, the advisor (who commented on the faulty dashboard) slowly glanced up past the motorcade and saw a faint light flicker against a window pane of one of the taller buildings. He took out a pair of binoculars to clarify the image. There was an opening at the bottom of the window, with a small hole beneath. It looked ominous...

... for that was where the alien gunman was hiding.

'Mr President,' he shouted, 'Get down, get down, get your head down!'

The President chuckled, 'Why, are we dancing?'

'No time to explain, sir, DUCK!'

'Are you calling me an ani-'

The advisor took vigorous action to save the President. He clamped his hand on the leader's neck and face-planted him down on the floor of the vehicle.

'OOOWWWHHH, MY NO-'

It did not seem to be the President's day to complete his sentences.

His wife turned her head in all directions, desperately tracking the alien assassin. The antenna hidden within the thick hive of hair, concealed inside a broad-rimmed hat, served their purpose, and she found him in the skylight. His swiftness was comparable to human instinct, like a gun duel of the Old West, but despite this, he missed the target. She joined her husband on the deck, as she was told by a *higher* source.

The shots fired out more formally, as a token, because the President's men already shielded him and his wife from the hostile firing. They rang out like an over efficient clock, and everyone realised what that meant...

... the negotiations were a hoax and the aliens just wanted to lure the isolationist President from his comfy home and garden, into the open.

Yet alas (for the aliens), the attempt had failed, and the headlines later read, 'PRESIDENT JOX SURVIVES ASSASSINATION ATTEMPT (and All He Got Was a Broken Nose)'.

The President lived on...

He raised himself to the seat, rubbing his head. His nose had bled, and his other hand held a makeshift tissue from the skirt of an over elaborated fashion of the wife.

The advisor asked if he was alright.

'Of course I'm alright,' came the curt answer.

A trickle of blood from a nostril was all the President suffered. It was a better option than the 'brains-upon-the-lane' one.

His wife by this time, had gotten up and dusted herself off, adjusting what was left of her skirt.

'I saw it coming,' she said.

The advisor freaked, 'You WHAT???'

'Yeah, I knew this would happen. Brilliant sunny day in downtown Ohnassah and going for a drive...,' she mused.

'You could have warned us of the threat, Mrs President.'

She muttered something odd, when the advisor ripped off the broad-rimmed hat. The lady's hair was askew, and a small piece of wire had stuck out, which was quickly yanked out.

'OUCH,' she cried.

'SHIT, THIS GIRL'S AN ALIEN!!!'

President Jox turned wildly. 'And I married... *you*??'

'Oh, quit it, it's not so bad. At least we've come to no harm. We made it!'

'We made it?' He shook her, 'Do you realise what just happened? And you...' He fingered the hole where the antenna was once housed. He checked his finger. It was bleeding. His eyes bulged wide open, as he gaped at the remnant of his once-cherished wife.

Dismayed and sadder than a fatal bullet wound, he said, 'Awh, fuck, get me outta this car, NOW!'

With good fortune, the motorcade was made up of a multitude of vehicles. The President had bolted away from the wife, from one car to the next one, and commanded, 'GO!'

That car moved quickly away from the heyday of the moment, speeding into sub light and disappearing down the next bend. Meanwhile, a message was emitted from the President's vehicle, and a group of secret commandos, hired by the Novaterran Government, raced up the staircases of the buildings and checked the grounds to find that assassin.

The failed assassin had escaped the building at this point, only to receive firepower aimed at him from the Novaterran ground forces. He was well shot-up, and even his insectoid form had been revealed underneath the human epidermis. The First Lady was taken in by Novaterra to be tried for conspiracy. Unfortunately, another advisor to the President had shot her down too. No need to waste good taxpayer money on alien scum that tricks people into submission.

'That will teach them fuckin' Saturninons,' cussed a government agent.

'The plots against us are immense,' replied another, with fashionable paranoia.

'It cannot go on much longer. Our President will somehow end this conflict, freeing us from hostile infiltration.'

'Watch it,' another chimed in, 'We've got some here already, and they are no threat.'

'I hope you're right, for your sake,' said the first agent, 'No one can beat the alien menace.'

The agents joined the President to HQ, where the rest of the motorcade met up.

There was no time to rest; the news of the assassination attempt spread far and wide; many Novaterran Free Press reporters from the region held a vigil to await the President's return...

... and pounced quickly as he got there.

'Mr President, Mr President,' they all scrambled for attention. 'Will you end the War? What about Novaterra's future? Will we be all in the clutches of the aliens? How can we defend ourselves?'

'The negotiations fell through. I do not know what's next,' came his reply, 'But, I will advise one thing. When someone tells you to duck, he means DUCK!'

He walked away in haste, his advisors protecting him like an oppressive umbrella.

A young blonde woman in her early 20s waited. She wore a badge which gave her name as Sharon. She eagerly approached the President.

'Mr President, sir,' she asked in a small voice. 'I heard about what happened. Are you okay?'

He turned to her and smiled, 'I most certainly am. Pity about the First Lady, though.'

'Why?'

'She turned out to be an alien transmitter.'

'Oh. Were you scared?'

'Agitated. Dammit, you can't even trust someone from your own bedroom! But, thank you for your refreshing honesty. At least you had the nerve and courage to ask how I'm doing, after all that. Everyone else wants to shove a microphone in my face and ask about the War.'

'That's too bad. I'll remember what you said.'

She shook his hand, turned and walked away.

'I'll remember your concern,' he called back.

She waved, blushing and went to her boring desk-jockey job at the school newspaper.

Another blonde woman approached and embraced him. She was a dear friend, much older than Sharon (by a decade or so), but still held high elegance. Sort of like the First Lady, only without antenna. *This one was fully human.*

'Jox, Jox,' she tearfully cried out.

'Buxloe. She was an alien.'

The two looked at each other like it was an eternity.

'Happy Birthday, Mr President.'

PHILIP TIMOTHY DAYE

CHAPTER I

I sat on my usual stool in my usual tavern, *The Winded Nest*, when news of the attempted assassination came through on the TV at the bar. I sipped and slurped my way through a few beers on my day off. I was on furlough, as a pilot of the Nuconnalow Squadron, fighting this near-millennial War against the aliens. I didn't like it. No one did. Except the aliens. They would pound and pulverise us and our allies.

A tune had played on the whirly-box. It was the latest song by the alien poet Jim-DugZek called *The Old Man in Paris*. DugZek was one of many of our allies, and wrote poems and songs for us to remember during these crazy times, the refrain went something like this:

The Old Man in Paris
Existing to survive.
Bloated as a toad,
His mind screams to unload
The latest song,
Untold.

I paid no thought to this teeny bop junk that people made and threw at the airwaves. I *rode* the airwaves, baby! I couldn't underestimate the popularity of such nonsense, though nonsense it was to me. It was as widespread as alien goo across the bow of a star ship. They put DugZek and others like him on a pedestal, only to give us hope...

... and when I said hope, I meant it for *all* of us.

I couldn't even fault the mindless tunes of the period. It took the mind away from the War: political machinations, government ploys and spies, and most of all, the trickery of the aliens attacking us. Everyone wrote songs with a strong effort, and DugZek's latest instalment was no exception.

Bands formed everywhere, even on different planets, depending on whose side you were on. Most of the tunes were propaganda stunts, but they sure made you feel good.

It was a fair day in the spring of 3168. A window curtain floated in captivity against the darkened walls of the bar area. The sun uncovered itself wide earlier and stepped up to play ball. Except it was *its* ball. The ghostly waves had many hours to unlock, yet it was still midday. It wasn't an easy morning for me. Nothing was easy for me. Being off flight schedules, relaxing, had disrupted my normally rigorous energy.

I had a small meal consisting of a sandwich, chips and the beer I was working on earlier. It tasted good. The tavern tried to accommodate more Earth-bound tastes and the Novaterran people's memories flooded the Silardian staff with ideas to make the place feel like home...

... *their* home.

I found it weird that the War allowed for exceptions. I never liked aliens, though refused to display prejudice against them. They were just targets or servants to me; nothing to go further than that. I admired the ones who were our allies. Some proved otherwise. I didn't care. I just wanted this damn War over with, so I can get back to doing normal stuff like flying overhead to track down criminals, or aerial photography. Flying landed you in many a job, and if you were lucky, you could make a keen living from it.

I was single. Still. Why? I never bothered to ask. I never bothered to look, chase nor settle. I just served the Novaterran Government and was proud to do so. There were plenty of women around, all flinging themselves at me as if I were some kind of hero. I was. They were proud of my flight missions, and picked up trash, which went toward fuel.

They also picked up more trash and put them into recycling bins to be refashioned as weapons against the aliens. It was funny to watch them do it, but most of the time, they remained very bashful about this. They did not like others watching them do it. I guess the concept of being 'lady-like' had reached these future times.

I spat into a nearby spittoon, and grabbed a cigarette from my pocket. I lit up and relaxed some more, breathing away the waves of a flightless day. A Silardian rinsed out the spittoon and placed it beside me. He figured I would need it again. I thought about family; my mother and father. My father was Rickert Conna Daye, a star pilot who fell long ago. I knew him, just. My mother Loretta Haze, had passed away, after my birth as Philip Timothy Daye in 3127; her name was soon forgotten. It was easy to forget when alien fire blasts through your neighbourhood. It made for a rotten day in the neighbourhood.

I was orphaned at 12, and raised by the State. At first, they tried to get surrogate parents who had no children, to emulate the beauty of parenthood. They didn't succeed. A normal feeling of security was given to me by the surrogates, but with them being partially allied-alien, I couldn't relate. Frustrated, I wanted to know my parents, or at least who I was. I went to the archives to search for my family, the Dayes. The hits went back three millennia! I had no time to look through every blessed entry. However, I found a fellow who was hybrid of human and Androsian called Hueriel Timodonnis Oconnadron Daye, descending from a Timothy Daye, an Earthman. I was part of that lineage. I read that a descendant of this Hueriel Daye (called Timconnah Daye), had left Andros IV near the beginning of the War to live on Novaterra. Many Androsians were human sympathisers leaving Andros behind, and Timconnah Daye was no exception (because he was partly human). I wondered about this human side from the Earthman Timothy Daye.

I checked further and there were loads of people from Earth with names similar to his, and all called Daye. Their origins were in Oconnalow, Ireland, and the history dated back to ancient Earth times to a royal couple called Muffyhuer and Cindihan. It stated the town was renamed in their honour, posthumously. Their demise was unknown; I heard they became the ground you walked on. In the Celtic mystical world of fairies, fantasies and dirt, anything could have happened. It was rather primitive and this didn't appeal to my futuristic 32nd century attitudes.

I closed the book and moved on with my life, but in those old records, I realised I had something to fight for. At least I had a past, and I carried it within me. The union and oddball end of the royal couple had started the Daye family. Before he died, Dad talked about them as if they were god-like. I didn't believe him; I'd bet they were dumbfucks like you and me. They just got lucky, that's all. Dad didn't respond, and later, joined the forces to become a pilot. In my good time, so did I, once the State got hold of me.

With all the reveries inside me, I re-spat into the spittoon and left it, with all the garbage behind.

CHAPTER II

I walked out of the tavern after surrendering some coinage to the barkeep. My mind reamed in thought still and I glanced at a news kiosk. The papers just broke the headline in Nuconnalow about the President's near miss this morning. I wanted to read it, so I paid the attendant, took the paper and myself to a nearby bench to read. I lit another cigarette. What fascinated me was that the aliens wanted a truce of some kind, which would end this stinging conflict; it would also release me from armed service. It was even odder to find the First Lady was a transmitter, an alien spy, driven just to lead the President on, and on toward a possible death.

That cigarette proved itself at the end of its link, and I stubbed it out with my booted foot. I exhaled some residue smoke, as I noted the quick thinking of the staff in the President's car at the time; how one word saved our leader's life...

...DUCK!

It was amazing how fate intervenes on small fry like us. I put the paper down for a bit, and looked around the small town of Nuconnalow. It was founded centuries ago, in the early days of the War, as a nod to the original name of Oconnalow, where the Dayes came from, and who so named it. It was a quaint name and a rightful homage. The ancient royal couple would now be immortalised in outer space.

I lived here all my life, and the pride so begins. I got up and took my thoughts for a walk. There was no panic or seriousness. People went on with their business like there's nothing going on. I enjoyed the lull. It calmed the mind. I saw more women. Wow. Some were cute, and some were quite the looker. I whistled to them in my mind and saluted them in reality. They gestured back, but didn't run wildly, asking for my autograph.

I experienced many girls in my forty plus years, but most of the relationships were meaningless. I cared, but not that much; they felt the same way. It was just a brief companionship.

Luckily, women did have more going for them in these times, with a shot at the services, just as the men were. The ancient women's movement of the latter part of the 20th century saw to that, albeit slowly. Now, anyone was game. Pretty blondes, redheads, brunettes of all shades and shapes sailed on a rainbow of victory. *Well, they hoped they did.*

I had time with them, even with aliens who were sympathisers to humanity. I could never remember the Latin-named species of aliens that crawled around the galaxy. No one could. It was said that a human broad called Lear had allied herself with aliens we referred to as the Blob People. They were the Valastron species, renamed for our humorous benefit. It was further said that her sob-story life had led to this War in the first place. I remembered from the archives about that Androsian half-caste Daye marrying an Earth woman called Shonnen, who was distantly related to Lear. *Damn, that means I had a close link to this shit!* I was glad this revelation didn't stick to me, nor damage my career and reputation as a decent human being. But it made me sick.

I came across some ladies in another squadron who took immediate interest in me; I was most grateful for the diversion.

'Ooooh,' one called Rigrah squealed, 'Is this pilot Daye of the Nuconnalow Squadron?'

I blushed. 'Yes.'

'Nicely done. Your skills are a boon to us all,' her comrade, Windt, extended her hand out to me.

As I shook hands with her, another cohort, Brieson, cried, 'You busy tonight?'

I cheekily asked her, 'Willing to fill yourself with me?'

She got all giggly, and handed me a book for me to sign. I gladly did.

'Thanks, Daye,' Windt said, 'Let's go girls.'

The women then left me for the next Big Thing. What that would have been, I could not foresee. Fame was fickle, as the saying went, but I still wondered if Brieson was busy tonight. I walked away from the hubbub in thought once more. That group were stunning. It was comforting to know that long ago, many ailments had been improved upon and we gave our minds more capacity for further use. Some of us didn't take advantage of it, some did. All and all, we were still dumbfucks, but at least we were better for it.

Alien women were still alien to me. They had odd habits that were difficult to get used to. Many had human-like qualities, but with a superior mindset. I called them snobbish, but their habits brought them down a bit. They drank with their ears or nose. Their orifices were placed differently to ours. Their sex lives must have been mind blowing. I've got on that ride before, but once over, you'd look at it and think *not again*, and move quietly beyond it in your moment.

I've had a woman once. A wife. Maybe three. I couldn't recall. The duress of war was repugnant, and it made me forget who they were and what they wanted out of me. But there was one girl who I had hooked on, and considered a basic interest in...

... the Silardian called Timithia.

The War drew all sorts, but unlike a comic book, this was real life. Timithia was tolerable by my standards. The Silardians were humanoid, with orifices in all the right places, waif-like and adept at cooking. I always valued someone good in a kitchen, and her race exceeded themselves. She lived on Novaterra for some time before I met her. She looked young, possibly my age, give or take a year or two, or a decade for all I care. It didn't seem like a bad match. Her eyes were earthen brown; rich like dark coffee, much needed on a tired morning. She wasn't tall, and blended in with the masses, as her alien-ness didn't diminish her look. She sided with us humans and worked in a local commissary, alongside other Silardians employed in the kitchens.

When I met her, she served me a pleasant meat dish, and gave me a fair smile. Her teeth were well-shaped, with a tinge of yellow in the pigment.

'It's from all the tea I drink,' she said.

'No bother. I'm into coffee myself, but I'd share a teapot with you anytime,' I showed her mine.

'Oooh, just like my teeth, cool,' she oozed (not literally, though).

We sparked off each other through my short meal. I later asked if I could see her again.

She seemed enthused. 'Where at?'

I sniggered at her catchphrase. 'How did you learn that?'

She gave me a look, pointing out her environment.

'Okay babe, I get it.' I swung near for a hug. 'Guess I'll pick you up and we can find something to swing at in Nuconnalow.'

She accepted.

So we made a date. Whoopee!!

CHAPTER III

Later that night, I stopped by her home on Jossi Lane, Bride's Crest. It was a small area consisting of sundry shops, a tavern (much like the one I go to), and a church, filtered in among the houses outlying the township. It was a quiet street that didn't go anywhere and Thia's house was at the end of it.

I went up to her place and knocked on her door. A small lace curtain flicked away in the side window, to reveal her smiling face. She waved at me and the door opened. I walked in. Her home was as tidy as she was. She lived alone. There were no familial portraits around, and everything was sparsely placed in the apartment. I reckoned her family must have been out of her life by now; most of them probable victims of the War or other things.

'Hey girl,' I cooed at her. 'How're ya doin'?'

'Okay, I guess.'

I looked around. 'You could make this joint more lively, you know.' I then broached the subject of family to her, wondering why the lack of photos or something.

Instantly, she read my mind and got defensive. 'They thought I was a bug person, like that family!'

Oh shit, what have I done?

'We're going on a date, dear, 'tis no time to cry over a spilled-away past.'

Her eyes welled as she gazed at my sunshine face. I could tell she needed a helping hand. Silardians were mostly self-sufficient, but this specimen was *clearly* in need.

I knelt down in front of her and put my hands on her lap. 'What can I do for you?'

'It was awful,' she cried out with a loud embrace, 'That family were evil people. They...'

'I thought you were a Silardian.'

'I am, but I was raised as a Saturninon, an alien bug species. The grandparents were from a human colony on Germus and caused issue in the town they lived in. The townsfolk drove them away, they couldn't tolerate their disservice during these times of conflict. They left Germus; in their flight, they discovered an amulet, which had shape shifting powers. It allowed them to change into whatever they wanted to be. For some oddball reason, they chose to be Saturninons, to make their escape from the human colony final. They turned away from their human form and all that went with it, to become that vermin-enriched bug people; the most hated species in all the system!'

'Oh dear, but at least you're a human Silardian.'

'Or a Silardian human; take your pick. I had a DNA test done to be certain, and it showed nothing but human and Silardian strains. My natural father was a Silardian. My mother was, you know...'

'A humanoid turned bug?'

She winced. 'Yeah, but at least she was pretty, else Dad wouldn't have fallen for her.'

'Ever met him?'

'No. The grandparents prevented the relationship from going any further. After I was born, they forced him to divorce their daughter. Then they took custody of me, and went as far as adoption to legalise their intentions.'

'Yeeech,' I moaned.

'It was against my human rights, which were denied to me because *they* chose to be bug people. I later discovered the amulet and reported it to the authorities. I had the pleasure of disposing the damn thing into one of the recycling foundries here. Its power is no longer upon me, nor is that adoption. Once they were found as phoney and even treasonous, the entire family were sent down for life. I heard they died in prison, as even prisoners have their pride and patriotism. You would die in prison too, if you're a human pretending to be alien. It does not go down too well during wartime.'

'No it wouldn't,' I agreed, and hastily changed topic. 'Hey, wanna go out to eat and have a dance or two?'

'Sure.' She got up to get her coat. 'I'm sorry I gobbed on you like that. I don't like discussing this stuff with people. I only did it to answer your question and you seemed nice enough, so...'

'That's okay, honey.' I slipped behind her and gave her a kiss. 'You needed someone to talk to.'

'So you won't call me a bug, or whatever? Everyone else did, once my origins were discovered. An incident happened at work, see...'

'What's it their business?'

She shrugged her shoulders. 'I dunno.'

'Anyway, you know the truth now.'

'I guess personal information is more scrutinised these days. Whose side you're on and all that.'

'Yeah. I reckon you'll be alright. You're still employed yes?'

'Eh. Someone started shit with me and I got into a tumble for it. They held my bug past against me, and I was close to leaving.'

My eyes widened. 'That's unfair.'

'Someone else in management thought so too, and fired the other person on the spot. I was left to carry on my job.'

'At least you don't look like a Saturninon.'

'No. The amulet's destruction dissolved any reference to it. I even got my name changed back to my original one.'

I turned to her as I walked out the door. 'What was that?'

'Silardicus.'

'You're a true blood Silardian if I ever saw one.'

We headed for a tram to the lights of downtown Nuconnalow. It was eerie, like Christmas, but it wasn't this time of year. That was where the eeriness came from. Lights flickered multicoloured patterns in the air. Buildings looked fashionable in celebration of their architectural magnificence. Thia and I got off the tram and swung into a revolving doorway which led to a dining and music club, *Thax.*

It was hidden in a silent nook at the edge of the main strip; dim enough for ambience and loud in compassion. I said compassion because the music was not as loud as some other venues in the area. Many folk here were older, and preferred a more quieter setting, to spark off the raucous setting of the young.

A popular crooner named Freedom-Bell Ock sang strong ballads; some tinged with remorse. Couples got up to dance, with some wallflowers getting menial attention from the notes. Thia and I danced along with the others. I looked closely at her and gave her a kiss. I wanted to make our moment last. The dance lasted quite awhile, as Freedom-Bell spoke in song:

I scream your name aloud,
Indiscreet,
As if you were a naughty treat.
Cos you're within the better part of me.
The gaslights went out in the street;
Determined, I was, to alight every one,
As I surrendered to your kind
In the violent wilderness below.

We took our seat in the dining area of *Thax*, where we had a fine Earth-style meal. On a cold day, you can have perpetual stew. Today was one of those days, even if it were night-time.

'Nice place,' Thia complemented my choice.

'Venue's good. I'd heard about it awhile back, but didn't want to go alone. I wanted to share it with someone special.'

Her crowded jealousy entered the fore. 'Who?'

'Duh,' I sassed back, 'YOU!'

'Oh,' she accepted my answer and took out a cosmetic implement. She gave her face a bit of a buff before returning the implement to her bag. Then she just looked at me.

I retorted, 'You and make-up do not make good bedfellows, do they?'

'Guess it is just getting with it, I suppose,' she sighed. 'I move with the times.'

'Yeah,' I smirked.

The stews and drinks arrived and we prepared to eat. I huffed a quick grace, then dived in. The stew was good and the hot toddy accompaniment was well worth it. It wasn't long before we finished and wanted to slow dance again.

Music was now playing through a whirly-box in the meantime, to give Freedom-Bell a break. He too danced, with a lady who resembled a raven on a wooden floor. His inner hand, tattooed by fiery will, and endless guitar playing, meshed kindly with hers. We danced the night away and soon, I fell into fondness for Thia, despite the sob story she'd shared with me earlier. True, it was my fault for that, and I swore never to bring that distress up with her again.

She noticed my eyes, and thought aloud, 'So you're into me?'

'Sure. I grab ya, dig ya, and think highly of ya.'

'Thanks,' she blushed. 'I hope I don't disappoint.'

'Nah, you swing coolly high.' I smiled at her.

More questions flew past me. 'You live near here? Alone, perchance?'

'Not far,' I replied with a grin. 'Hey, while I'm on leave, can I see you again?'

'I'd like that. You can meet me at that commissary where I work.'

'Can do. Will do,' I assured her.

When our little festivities ended, we took the tram home to her place. She needed to get settled, so she can return to work in the morning.

'Want a nightcap or something,' she suggested.

'Ummm, yes,' I answered, thinking: *yeah, the prospect!* 'Coffee would be good.'

'That'll keep you spinning yarns all night. How about a liquored chocolate.'

'Whatever,' I croaked, thinking rather rudely at her offer.

She brought out my drink and sat next to me.

I wondered, 'Where's yours?'

'I took a flavoured tranqua-pill,' she answered, 'It's like a morning vitamin, but for night-time use. I've been having bad spells lately.'

That vow I made to myself earlier came to fruition, and I changed the subject. 'Want me to stay with you? I do have a place of my own, temporary of course, but it'd be lonely as hell.'

'I agree,' she said. 'Stay.'

After I'd done myself with that chocolate drink, I shifted the sofa cushions and made myself comfortable under the drooping blanket that covered the top of the sofa.

Thia stared blankly at me. 'Uh-uh.'

I responded. 'Uh-uh?'

She shook her head. 'Uh-uh.'

She headed for the stairs.

Damn, it was only our first date. Yet, with the War still on, love had no time to take time. We could all die in seconds. *Alone!*

I took her grunted advice and raced to catch up to her. After washing up, we were soon together, under *her* blanket.

She asked, 'Cosy in here?'

'Ummm,' I closed my eyes and smiled.

We kissed goodnight and I rolled over to sleep. It wasn't going to be *that* kind of date.

CHAPTER IV

The next morning, my arm extended outward to an empty space. I freaked out in fear and jerked up instinctively. Thia was already up and dressed.

She smiled back at me. 'You didn't think it would be *that* kind of night, did ya?'

I hadn't looked my best, and needed a shave. 'No I didn't.'

'Very well, then. I've gotta go to work. You can lock up. The door's on auto, so you don't need the mortise.'

'Okay,' I smiled. I enjoyed her no-nonsense sensibility. Not like she'd give me the key to her place, much less the key to her heart!

She left me alone in her apartment. What a risk she took, but it wasn't like there was anything to take in the first place. *I just wanted her.* I liked her a lot... possibly bordering on love. Any girl will do, and I loved the once-enslaved special cases. Normal women were boring. Thia was different. And she deserved better. And furthermore, why not a hot star pilot like me, fighting for freedom, blowing up aliens? I could shoot them down, just as well as Freedom-Bell could sing them down.

I got dressed into my yesterday clothes, as I slept in my underwear. Sleeping in underwear was fine, but I desperately couldn't wait to change.

Later, I closed the door and went back to my place in a local hotel, the Klaaxon in Sydmouth. Everyone bunked-up there. It was on the way to Fort Lynchner, where I was stationed. The desk clerk gave me a letter before I went upstairs to my room.

Firstly, I took care of my needs. Shower, shave, dress. Eating could be done later.

I ripped the envelope open. It read:

Colonel Daye:
Your leave expires in 24 hours. Please report to Fort Lynchner at 0700 hours on Wednesday, 12 June.
CO Dexx

I threw the letter down and contacted Thia. I left a message on her phone. I left it at that. I hoped she'd get it.

I spent the day in silence and suddenness. My newly budding friendship with her was possibly doomed from the start. I couldn't let this happen. I felt saddened that I was to return to my work, and she would just play 'waitress' at a beaten down old commissary, when instead, *I could have her all to myself.*

Thumbs twiddled nervously, when soon the phone rang. My heart went into my brain and took over.

I hastily answered, 'Thia, Thia.'

'Phil, don't be a bore,' she blurted. 'It's only the next day.'

'God no,' I cried, 'It's been eternal!'

'Oh please,' she dismissed. 'I got your message.'

'I'm leaving.'

'So I hear. How far is it to Lynchner?'

'A long search, as far as it goes, for all I care!'

'PHIL!'

'Okay, okay. It's outside Nuconnalow, past Sydmouth. You can't miss it.'

'I can still see you?'

'CO permitting. Dexx is reasonable, to a point.'

'This sucks. Let's meet up tonight. Your last night,' she suggested.

'Love to. I'll catch up to you on Jossi Lane and go from there.'

'Okay. Gotta go. Bye.' She rang off.

Tears flooded my eyes with hope as I put the receiver down. I thought about technology for a second, and how it all seemed so backward, like we were living a millennia ago. The War had taken its toll on our progress; we were living in a makeshift earlier epoch of our own making, just to survive. At least we didn't resort to rotary dialling.

I started to pack up, ready to report to Dexx tomorrow. I was furious about it, yet the ye old pooper-scooper of life dealt me a large heaping mess to clean up. *And it was filthy!* In these uneasy times, with alien blasts and primitive survivalist lifestyles, it was a wonder we were all still alive. I thought about hitching the stars, and getting Thia in on my action. I wondered if she'd go for that. Hmmm, it would beat being alone. We didn't have much time, either. You didn't know if you were going to go or not. *It wasn't worth the wait.*

Night came and I proposed immediately. No ring. Just plain, makeshift haste.

'Will you marry me, Thia?'

'Sure,' she replied deadpan, 'When?'

She accepted. SHE ACCEPTED!

'I don't know,' I cried without thinking, fearing for all to see. 'Maybe there's a hitching post Dexx didn't tell me about. We could pull our fort straps together.'

'Sounds romantic,' she cooed. 'Who's Dexx?'

'My CO.'

She gave a look.

'Commanding Officer.'

'Ah,' she shook her head.

We later went out and shared the bed back at her place.

'I could always stuff the commissary job and work at Lynchner for our cause,' she said aloud.

'Could do, yeah. They're always looking for help. You being a Silardian shouldn't be a problem.'

'What about the bug past?'

'I'll deck Dexx if he fucks with you about it. You're my wife-to-be. He'll understand. You'd make a good change.'

'I thought military meals were supposed to be bland.'

'Who said you had to work in the kitchens?'

'That's what I'm good at.'

I looked at her with a gleam in my eye. 'A soldier, flyer, or diver is worth a thousand decent Silardian made meals, especially if it were to be his last. I know you're good at it, but you could be more.'

'Like what?'

'Telecommunications link.'

'Yeah, and I can link up to my home planet.'

'Har-har,' I sniggered loudly at her. 'And you can shut your little trap and do what I say.'

'You suggested it.'

'I want to see more of what you are.'

She began to remove her nightwear.

'Hey, wait a minute, I didn't mean it like that,' I screamed.

She looked normal to me.

'I'll keep praying for you. I know you may go on a final mission. Every mission is a final mission, until you turn up the next day or so,' she added.

She clasped her hands into mine and together, we slipped into a silent robe, savouring a spiritual moment together.

She kissed me. 'There's one for the road. I look forward to being Mrs Philip Daye.'

'You would. Oh, this is groovy, my baby.'

I think I spilt too many beans that night. Luckily, the lass was covered.

We embraced and kissed, but it didn't last long.

The morning came too soon, and I had to scoot outta here. *Fast.*

'I'll contact ya,' I called, fleeing out her door.

'Bye, Phil.' She waved gravely, as she got ready for work.

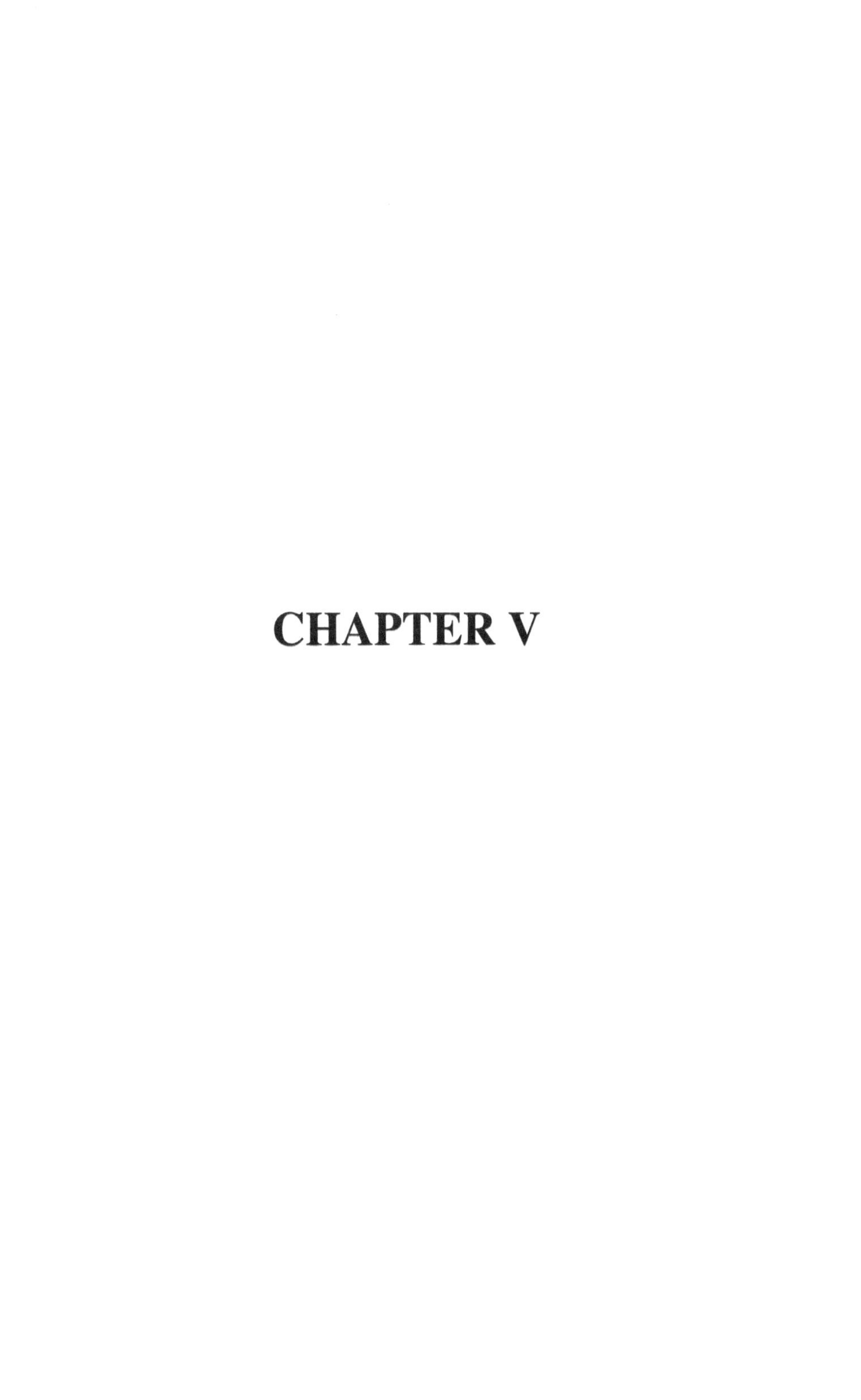

CHAPTER V

The morning tram ride back to base was uneventful. People sat around like living zombies, festering through their breathing day. Some could've used some coffee; I certainly did. Soon my stop was nigh, and it was time for me to get off. So I did and walked a few blocks toward a castle-like fortress that awaited me. It wasn't all that; a large edifice housed dorms, meeting rooms, kitchens and an airstrip on the side of the layout, to alight your path to glory.

I missed Thia already, and soon I was at Lynchner's threshold. *Gee, it wasn't such a long search after all.* More like a small tram ride further downtown to the edge of Nuconnalow.

A private lackey greeted me. It was Jarris.

'Dexx wants you,' he announced, 'He wants you BAD.'

'Okay, okay, no need to hustle about it,' I scoffed.

Jarris did an abbreviated four-step shuffle before returning to quarters.

I then entered Dexx's realm. His office was well worn, somewhat lived in, and made comfortable. For the CO. For anyone else, it was negligible.

He asked straight up, 'So, how was your leave, Daye?'

'Fine. I met a girl the other day. I think I'm in love. Thia. Timithia Silardicus.'

'A Silardian? Oooh, you're getting experimental, Daye.'

'She's half human, and on our side,' I defended.

'Well, that can't be all that bad. Some aliens have been generous with our hospitality. Others, well,' Dexx sighed, 'It's the bugs and blobs I hate the most. The problem with them is they throw their disgraceful, ugly ooze down the pavement. They make a slick-shit mess. Hard to clean up, too, so I'd watch it, Daye. You may be in for it with your Thia, as you call her.'

My cheeks were a-flush from the presentation of attitude he displayed. I sighed too, lamenting about Thia's buggy past, but in keeping to my personal vow, I withheld that part of her life. As her DNA was verified as Silardian and human, there was no real comment to make upon her. How you're raised does not reflect in records...

... if it did, records could be changed, *or destroyed...*

... and I think Thia took care of all that, I hoped.

'She's true to our cause and our ways. Our freedom and hers.'

'Hers? What is she, a refugee or refuse?'

My blue eyes widened to meet with Dexx's. 'WHAT? We're all in it together. I was just speaking for her in her absence. I trust she wants freedom as well.'

'We all want fucking freedom, but we all have to fight for it.' Dexx then changed the subject, 'Anyway, Daye, you've got a flight mission coming up. It's voluntary but it will put you to work, to make up for your recent inactivity. You up for it?'

'Yes sir,' I shouted and saluted firmly in militant character. But then, I began to blubber, 'I wanna get married!'

'COLONEL DAYE,' Dexx shouted, 'Is that the way an officer behaves? *Naughty Daye.* Imagine what the aliens would make of us, if they found out we're all lily-livered inside. That won't do, even within a box of muenster cheese! You should be on report for your fuckin'-ass outburst, COLONEL. BUT... I won't, cause it ain't civil. *In order to preserve humanity, we must learn to be humane.* When do you want to marry?'

My eyes widened, surprised at another flick of attitude that harshly brushed the air between us. 'Any time. Ummm, could you marry us?

Dexx showed repulsion. 'Eeeeck, and join y'all in a 'trois'? Hell no!'

'No, no, I mean do you have authority to wed us?'

Dexx laughed. 'Gotcha Daye. I was just pulling your leg, and arm, too. I can arrange for a universal chaplain to officiate. I ain't that powerful an official.'

'Yeah,' I argued back, 'But you can put someone on a life or death mission.'

'Don't take that tone with me, son. That is your job and don't you forget it. I'll get that jerpy Jarris to replace you.'

'He'll not come back in time.'

'Well, tough shit, Daye. If you want to marry, you'll do as I say. This is not a slumber-jive for all you flyboys, you know. *You're here to kick alien butt, not marry it.* But if you must, I'll provide the witnesses. Now what's it to be?'

Taken aback on the spot, I replied, 'I'll do it your way, sir.'

'Good. Go tell your girl it's okay to hitch. But I warn ya, Daye, watch it. The Silardian temper is an open hatchway to the clouds and I ain't going along that arc!'

'Thank you sir. You're wonderful,' I gushed loudly, and shook his hand.

'Well don't spread it, or no one will listen to me. Then chaos reigns and that is unacceptable when fightin' aliens.'

'Yes sir.'

It didn't matter about whether anyone listened to Dexx; soon, all of Lynchner was aflame with the news. Fellow pilots went up to congratulate me and get me high on booze during the off-hours. My time on base was lightened, now that Jarris was flying my mission; it consisted of a short-round of surveillance over Novaterra. Any enemy activity was to be reported, and taken down fast.

To increase the cause of celebration, some music had been played over the wireless speakers on the base. An ancient Earth song called *Indiana Wants Me* had blared, complete with the cops and robbers style sound effects embedded in the song. It was as valuable a tune, as molten metal was to a foundry, but not as portable. It turned out the klunkiness of the era showed when it was revealed the song was played from a collectable 45 single on a victrola. Someone was posted to record duty to change the records. It was tedious dealing with antiquated technology, but there was nothing like a flying archive to get you going. It was no different than the old radio DJs of the 20th century and beyond, playing tunes all day to keep the morale going. This was as vital as flying and killing aliens.

The record stopped, and a silence on the airwaves dug in to see what other items were stored. This change of record can be rather drawn-out.

Soon, another tune came on called 'The Golden Idol of Guyan':

Inside his tracks laid bare,
Long enough to care.
He was away in old station Paddington,
As a large boulder rolled there,
Erasing what's unfair.

Everybody hee-hawed about the illicit jokes and funfair news my upcoming marriage made. Announcements roared over the tannoy. Nothing rude was said, though many hip-hip-hoorays were belted out in my name.

Once I got into DJ mode, it was my turn to thank everyone for their kindest sentiments. I played some tunes that I cherished, even going as far as music meant for the younger set. I played DugZek and Freedom-Bell's records. I also dipped into 20th century tunes, as well as those made by the Lattice Wyndows in the early years of the War.

Meantime, people were shouting for victory and cleaning up the joint, recycling endlessly toward its sacred ends. The day wore on for me without Thia. I used the phone in the control booth to call her.

Brrring. Brrring. Nothing.

I left another message, and told her to get me at the base.

A few psychedelically-laced songs later, the phone rang.

'Thia?'

'Phil?'

'Ah, it's you at last,' I sounded relieved.

She asked, 'How're you doing?'

'Nothing. Playing records to keep up morale. Making clarion shouts about the place, and getting shouted back in return. You know the like.'

'Sounds like you told them.'

'I did.

'What did Dexx say?'

'Anytime babe, you name it.'

'Christ, ummm....how about tomorrow?

'Tomorrow's the 13th. Bad luck.'

I knocked upon the wooden desk.

She heard the knocking. 'You superstitious? In this century? God, you're lame.'

'Whatever. How about in a day or so?'

'The day after bad luck day?'

'Saturday, then?'

'This is all a bit sudden.'

'So's our love. Well???'

'I'll get back to you.'

DAMN!

She rang off. Her job was demanding, and I understood. However, if it were someone else, my doubts would surface quicker than a cross channel swimmer, after a long marathon.

I contacted Dexx. He called me back to his office.

'Geez, you hadn't even given me time to arrange things. Matrimony is still a big to-do,' he whinged.

'We ain't got time, sir.'

'You do, punk. You ain't a-flying, yeah? I gave that to Jarris, busting his behind on YOUR behalf. You can wait, dumb head.'

'Saturday?'

'No.'

'Next month?'

'Maybe.'

'DEXX!'

'Alright. Saturday it is. Gives us a few days to do shit. Bit short notice, but I can get one of the chaplains in town. They do rounds now and again, but they're pretty stationary normally.'

'Great. I'll tell Thia.'

'WAIT,' he ordered.

I paused. 'What?'

'Ain't you gonna thank and invite me?'

I relented. 'Thank you, Commander Dexx, and will you be my best man?'

'Hogwash, I'm the man for the job. Come here you big lug of soldier.'

We embraced in a brotherly manner, then I went to call Thia.

CHAPTER VI

Once I made the call to Thia, I did some light shift prep duties. Whoever was on base was good enough for ceremony and witnesses. The CO, Dexx, made preparations and called in his old friend Reverend Backnah. *He wasn't much, but he'll do*, Dexx thought. At least he was nice enough to spare his time away from our fighters. I know he didn't look the part, but in these strapped times, who does?

Thia had no one to invite. She thought she did, but memory relapses were a bitch and it turned out that most of her friends had died in endless hunger strikes for peace. She, of course, knew better. Yet, it doesn't detract the fact there was something to be done. So one of the fly girls, Windt, who was stationed on base, took her place next to Thia, and all seemed complete.

We were a ravishing pair, to say the least. In the short time we had to prepare for this, we had to reinvent things. Food had to be sourced, and it was our own cook, Brian, who made it possible to come up with things at short notice, such as a makeshift dinner from all the leftovers you could muster. Flowers were sent special delivery; they were sent via special post, and you had to pay a fair bit in that game. One of the other female officers had a cream dress, and it'd do nicely. Our rings were also under military jurisdiction: one of the late tech pilots had a ring, and she had small fingers like Thia, so her ring was equally attained.

Once all was gotten in the cooling operative flow, our wedding could begin. Everyone went outside, where all the seating was filled; they wanted to see the giant hotshot, Philip Timothy Daye wed Timithia Silardicus. At least it was what we came to, once we found the details of her early life, such as birth, adoption, and expulsion from family. We didn't let anyone in on it, and made sure Thia got the justice she deserved, even if backed up by the military.

The ceremony began, and I couldn't wait to have Thia. No one questioned, argued, nor wanted the sweet princess that was mine. Once the preliminary parts were read out, Backnah asked me:

'Do you, Philip Timothy Daye, take Timithia Silardicus as your lawful wedded wife; to have and to hold, until your eternities are set?'

I gushed, and didn't hesitate. 'I do.'

'Do you, Timithia Silardicus, take Philip Timothy Daye, as your lawful wedded husband; to have and to hold, until your eternities are set?'

'I do,' she blushed.

Backnah concluded, 'I now pronounce you man and wife. You may kiss the bride, Phil.'

I fell into a damn cool swoop, and got Thia where I wanted her. She gently kissed me, and we found each other most appealing. The good Reverend walked out for a breath of fresher air, as he left us to it.

The party commenced and carried on for a long time, into the evening. We got congrats from all sides, danced and frolicked, as well as spending much needed time together. Not that we needed much anyway. Sigh. I really was surprised, yet thankful for this moment.

Sometime later, Thia and I went on our honeymoon. It was a small village outside Lynchner, called Legaul, where we spent more time together. It was nice and quiet, and made much time for ourselves. We didn't even think about the War. Love was on the cards, and *we did a lot of that.*

When we returned, there was much to do. I relocated to base, where I posted to guard duty temporarily. I also did watch monitoring, in case the aliens had different ideas and would fester in or near our locality. Thia got out of her rented apartment and moved in with me, lock, stock and barrel. She went to work with us on base, as she was more than happy to leave her old job at the commissary she'd had for a few years. And it was getting tiresome. I hoped that what we provided wouldn't singe her too much. She had physical prowess, but not enough to fight. Her hands and shortened fingertips saw to that. Dexx put her on monitoring and intelligence duty. It adhered her to what was going on and it wasn't good practice to keep the good lady in the dark. *Don't care what anyone says to that!* It allowed her to find the aliens and left *them* guessing where we were.

A while onward, I found myself in my spacecraft on another mission. It was routine, but we needed to see alien activity from above, not just below. Once we made sure our perimeters were cleared, it allowed our ships to do their bit. I left the base, and flew to all corners of Novaterra.

I found nothing on my scanners, and nothing in the immediate jurisdiction either.

There was no activity, and reported it so. I made my report to Dexx and emailed it from one of the output ranges on the ship. I felt a blast of cool air from somewhere but didn't look to see outward. I flew my ship toward the coordinates of Vexes Nova. An asteroid just sat there, staring at me. My ship pattered and puttered along several trajectories, until...

... BLAM!

My ship hit the ground. It certainly wasn't Novaterra. *God, that was rough!*

Where was I? Too many questions kept coming to mind, as I landed, and released myself from the ship.

More questions came to the fore. What was this? Christ, this was a drippy, droopy laden atmosphere. Lucky I had my bio suit on. It was as dense as hard rock and internally solar-lit. *Ugh!* Some bugs came alive, peering their festered looks at me. They thought *I* was the enemy. They were right. But it didn't do to make your guesses at just *anyone*.

'You are correct,' a voice shrilled outward, as if reading my thoughts.

'Excuse me,' I responded. 'I just landed, I...'

'Silence,' the voice revealed a humanoid drone with a bug skeleton around it. It was creepy; you wouldn't want to mess with this, even on a sunny day.

I was speechless.

'You are from planetoid Earth colony Novaterra?'

'Yes,' I said.

'I am bug species 2469 of Saturnon. You are trespassing on our vortex. I will give you a few minutes to leave or you become my prisoner and meet Zenatour,' it said.

I looked around, parched in flight and thirst. I started making my way back to my ship to leave, when...

... another bug emerged, and zapped me with his ray gun. I then fell unconscious.

'Zen would be pleased at this,' one of the bugs commented.

'Take him on our ship. We've got a long travel ahead of us,' another answered, strapping itself in for takeoff.

Alone in a grapple hook, I became conscious, well, semi-conscious. I didn't think these guys would allow someone to be over stimulated, especially before meeting their Leader, Zenatour. The journey seemed a mere few minutes before we reached the main lair of *bugdom*. It was lonely though, considering most of the bugs were not talkative and doing their versions of what we would do, if it were the other way round. Their stable bodies held themselves high above others, they swelled in pride where it counted. They were good for one use, and that was the end of them. Afterward, new bugs hatched and took their place, killing off any bug that was of no further gain.

Once the ship got to its new port, I was taken to Zen's hideout on a cliff. It was cold, rocky and difficult to climb, if unprepared. Everyone was prepared naturally, and it made for a fleeting journey for me. Inside the cave, Zenatour sat proudly on the dais. He didn't make any friends, nor counsel with anybody around him, as they would all snuff it the one day or the next day, and there would be a new pestilence to deal with.

I was right to make judgment upon this misty cave of insects. It really grossed me out. Some were humanoid shaped, but don't let that fool you. Their minds were insectoid, and for the most part, it was obvious.

'Approach,' Zenatour spoke aloud, 'What or who do we have with us today?'

A newer leader flinched his noise particles at the rest. 'I've got a human from Novaterra.'

'A Novaterran? Well, well. Let me have a look at him.'

Zenatour left the dais to come to my side for a keen look. I was brought forth, bug-constrained, to the immense bug they referred to as their Leader.

He said, 'What is your name, then?'

'I am Colonel Philip Timothy Daye, no. 731927, sir.'

'Ah, a militant. We like militants, don't we?'

The bugs around Zen all agreed, flashing their 'teeth' about, in a vain attempt at smiling.

'I was sighting the asteroid for routine purposes.'

'As routine as you want to be,' Zen laughed, or sounded something like one anyway. 'You wish to demolish our bug worlds so you can procreate your geneticist-nonsense unprovoked, eh?'

'We just want to survive,' I argued, 'Novaterra saw to that.'

'Yes, it did,' the Leader reflected. 'Why were you sent here?'

No answer.

'I cannot hear you,' Zen called.

Still no answer.

The frustrated Leader put a hand on his face. 'Well, if you don't tell us, who will. And how do we know you won't stake your claim to this asteroid? You may do so, but at your peril.'

Zen continued to laugh at my gormlessness, and I took it all like a man. Though torture wouldn't work, it never did. What I did have proved indispensable...

... my mind.

I deflated all the agony I could take from the Bug Lord. What I put up with in my mind was pure genius. I knew it would bear fruit in good time. As the ray entered me, I doubled all my concentration on it. I thought about wild things, as well as tame. I thought of Thia, and the difficulties she had in her past. Her family were nothing compared to these razor driven bugs! I realised I could destroy the ray set upon me, and make a go for my gun (which was taken during my capture).

I waited patiently, threw a few curve balls down that alien's mind, then...

... WHALLOP!

I grabbed my gun, and shot everything coming toward me, and at me. I mowed down a few bugs, and kept running. Zen was totally bugged on the matter, to say the least, and had his best troops filing after me. I used everything I had, even telekinesis, which came in handy when needed.

As I finished off the last of them, Zenatour knew he'd had it, but laughed at the end. 'Your ship is on the far side. Board it as you wish; my men disabled it in more ways than one. It may take time for you to leave.'

The creature filed out, still laughing among his cohorts.

'Oh,' I cried aloud, 'I suppose you can fix it for me?'

'I could, if I want to,' came a chuckle-ridden answer.

The Leader put on an overcoat and pitter-patted out of range. No one on Earth or Novaterra could match this!

I found my way back to the ship. It was in tatters. God, it would take me weeks to put everything all back together! Parts of the ship were in heaps nearby, and as far out as a local riverbed. I took my time assembling it. Bugs watched me as I went over parts in disarray. They laughed at me as I was doing it. Some of them even pointed and spoke of *their* naked prowess on my ship!

Eventually, after days of this, I gave a very loud PHEW to the air, and left the desolate asteroid back to where it belonged. In a dung heap.

I now laughed, and as I began my way toward Novaterra, I knew it was fleeting. I knew it was flying. It was something I liked to call home.

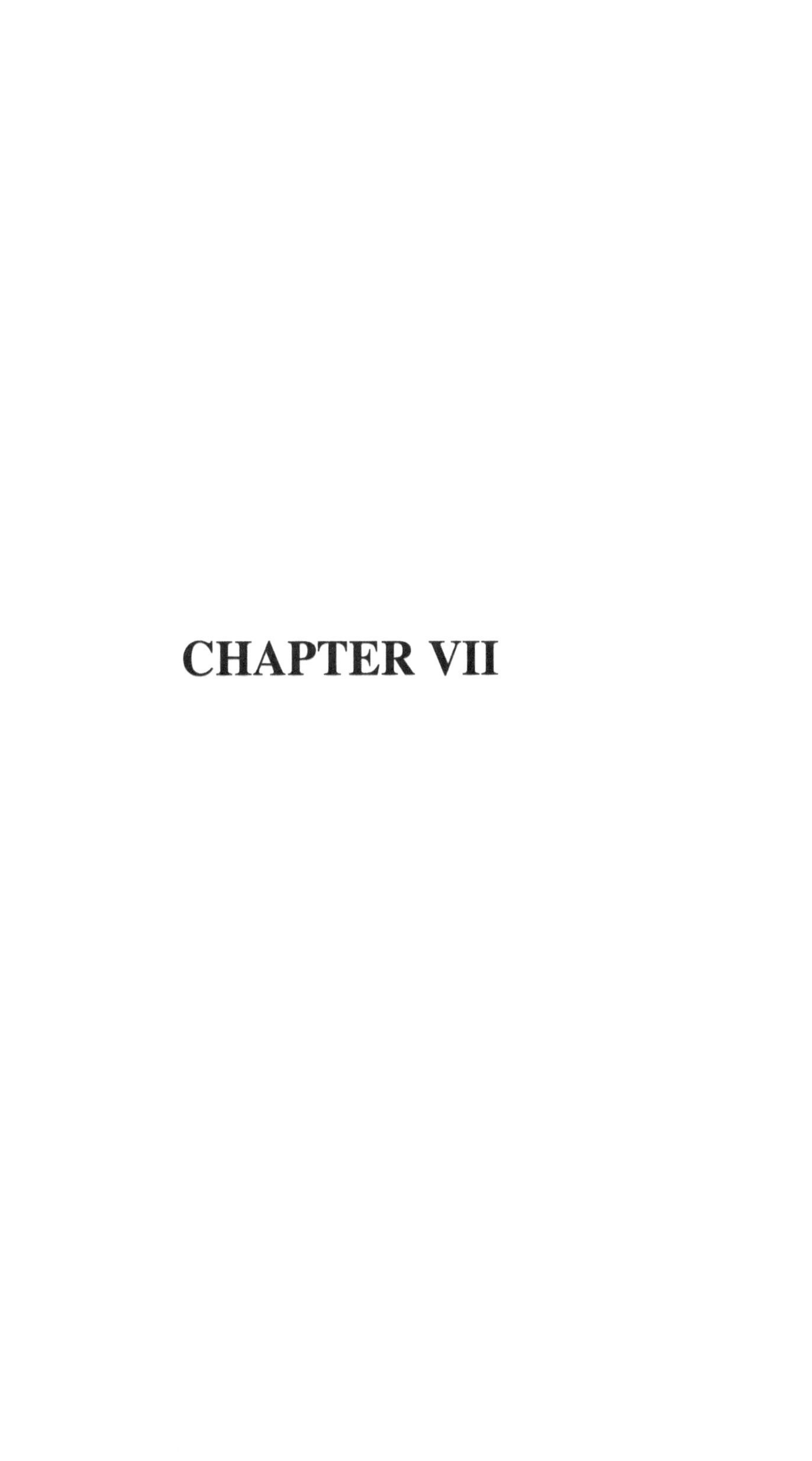

CHAPTER VII

When I returned to base, I was stunned by a greeting.

'Welcome home, Dad,' everyone called out.

Dad? Me? No way. I didn't think Thia was pregnant when I left. I didn't think I was away *that* long.

'Well, you were, Daye,' Dexx said, 'And we have a surprise for you.'

'What surprise,' I began to say when Thia came out with a rucksack. Inside the pretty frame was a baby.

'Oh?' I was amazed at the little bundle that greeted me.

'Phil,' Thia replied, 'Good to see you back. Now, have a look at this.'

'You're asking me, Thia?' I was thrilled when I reached in to pull the baby up. 'Oh, she is a darling.'

I cooed and ahhed, and Dexx wanted to throw up. But he didn't. He knew better. He knew better than to throw up with a baby on the base.

'Awh, she's real cute, Daye,' he said, 'Maybe we can program her to...'

I gave a forceful look at him. 'NO!'

'Well, I was just kidding. Who knows? Maybe she won't be involved with our war.'

I was dumbstruck, but not stupid. 'Wanna bet?'

The infant squealed and spat out gibberish. Sort of like English, sort of well, baby talk. I didn't know. She was typical of her few weeks on Novaterra, and came instilled with what there was to know. It just took time and development to drag it out. I felt very sure of my new daughter.

'We'll put you on light duty again, Daye,' Dexx commented, walking away, 'I don't want you going all manic for a hoosegow.'

I cried, 'What?'

'Never mind,' Thia put her hand on my shoulder. 'Dexx is just nuts. Enjoy your daughter. They can't put you on a deep probe this close to fatherhood.'

'No, I guess they can't.' I reached for a beer in the closest fridge.

'So how did it go?'

'Got entangled with Saturninons on a distant asteroid. Do you know they wanted to colonise further?'

'Course. That's why we monitor their distortions.'

'No taking where those spark plugs emerge.'

'It's worse when it hits your shores,' she added.

I was shocked. 'You mean?'

'Yes, Phil. They were here. We were able to repel them quickly before any damage could be done. They couldn't find anything to pursue us with.'

'I wasn't here.'

'I know,' she followed.

'Were they after me?'

'They were after anyone who would follow their deceptiveness.'

'Eeewwhh! I didn't think it was *that* bad.'

'It was. And it can come again.'

'What about the baby?'

She gasped, 'What baby?'

I gave her a duh look. 'That little girl you're carrying outside yourself?'

'Ah, you mean Cynthia. Yeah, she's cool, no?'

'Cynthia?' I reflected on the name. Good. Sounds like Cindihan, but close enough.

'I'm going for a nightcap,' Thia said. 'Want one?'

'Love one,' I answered, as that beer I had earlier was long gone.

We headed for our room, where we put the baby in her cot, and we just found ourselves surrounded by love, and a reasonable bed fill. A hot drink was also provided for, too.

'Phil,' Thia began, 'It's so good to see you again. I never thought it would happen.'

'What?'

'Well,' she got comfy next to me, 'Your leaving. You know how it is. We all have to be alert for aliens and next thing you know, you could be on another base in Novaterra.'

'Far away from this one?'

'Yes.'

I kissed her. The baby Cynthia was cooing in her blankets. Everything was right with the world. It seemed so far, and so gone. Nothing compared to this moment. The problem was Cynthia, though. She got up and walked in her cot to the outer ridges. She then stared at us intensely.

I soon cast my eye on her. 'What are you doing up young lady?'

'Goo,' said Cynthia, and then she sat down and cried, because she knew her game was up.

'No no no,' I called out, 'I didn't mean it, no, here.' I picked the child up and held her on the bed with Thia. She found quietude and enjoyed the scenery.

I eyed her calmly. 'What you think? I bet she'll blast aliens!'

'I think she'll blast the sky if put down to it,' Thia replied.

'Do you think she'll be happy with us?'

'I don't know,' she pulled a sheet across her chest, 'Ask her.'

'Wait a minute,' I hesitated, then looked at Cynthia. 'You don't think she's...'

'Say it Phil.'

'No.'

'Yes.'

'She's an early developer, as the old term goes,' I surmised.

'Yes Phil, she is. She's also talkative somewhat.'

Wow, a baby with a great mind and mouth. Now, this I'll have to see.

'Cynthia,' I spoke softly. 'Are you happy being with your parents?'

'Goo,' she eyed me, picking up on any slackness. 'Aaahhhggahhhh.'

'She's good,' I nodded.

'She's clever, but not in where we need her, yet,' Thia commented.

'We'll have a go then, shall we?' I picked up the young one, and made picky baby-talk faces at her.

Cynthia was delighted with my efforts and said something like, 'Where's now, Dad?'

I was stunned, and didn't expect *this*. 'Huh?'

'Where's now, Dad,' the baby repeated.

'I don't, I don't, I...,' I fainted in the blankets.

Thia got me up, but couldn't. She left me to talk to Cynthia.

Cynthia told her, 'You might have warned him.'

'I did,' Thia snapped, 'I didn't think you'd make a show for it.'

'A show? What do you think this is? Here I am, fresh born; fresh bored, more like, and you two start acting like I have no mind!'

'In reality, you're not supposed to.' Thia sighed, 'I guess it's time for you to meet Dexx.'

The child shook, 'Why?'

'Maybe you can help us track down alien species, prevent them from infiltrating with our cultures.'

'Yeah, okay,' Cynthia noted. 'Where's Mr Floppy, then?'

Thia pronounced, 'Who?'

'My bear-cat thing?'

'Oh,' the older woman looked hastily around, then came across it. 'Found him.'

'Oh goody,' Cynthia reached out her hands to her oddly mixed animal.

She spent the rest of the night sighing and cooing to herself, while asleep on the divan next to us. Her crib was her last delight.

'Phil,' Thia called out.

I got up hastily. 'What?'

'The child's asleep now. I'll put her away, and we can begin again.'

Thia took the child back to her cot. She covered her up in her blanket.

'Good night Mummy,' the child said, with omnipotence.

'Good night,' sighed the frustrated mother.

Thia walked away and joined me. 'Well, shall we?'

'Don't mind if we do,' I grabbed a remote and we watched a late night film.

Once it ended, we were out, and dozily, I switched off the channel. At times, aliens could catch you out on electronically. I could not take that chance with my family.

CHAPTER VIII

As the days wore on, my duties in honour increased, as little Cynthia grown too. I taken to calling her Cindy, as we named her for her near-namesake Cindihan. I got to enjoy a good taste of fatherhood, with some other staff looking after her while I performed in my station.

Cindy was now three, and Thia noticed no serious change in the child. All she did was the usual childish murmurings and occasional banter which no one really paid much attention to. *She was only three!* It wasn't much at first. Thia fed the little girl many things ranging from pure dietary mush to some solids. Fresh vegetables, meats, cheeses, yoghurts, and other things made it to Thia's hand blender. When it becomes a smooth paste, it was most palpable for little mouths to feed on. Now, she was on solids for life and it was accepted by her, as the food wasn't any different from what she was getting in the past. Only it was proper food, and not, well, mush!

Playing alone in our room was rather challenging for the little mite. Playing with large plush and plastic toys could only go so far, as Cindy became more adventurous in her field. She still allowed the practices Thia had provided her. It reminded me of my days as an infant, growing into a toddler, into the child and man I've become. I didn't remember *everything* of course, but for much of the time, it was good. It was a questionable time though, because most children this age and a year or two later go into the outside world more, and grow beyond the limitations of home. Nurseries and day centres were much in vogue at this time, but not with us. We decided to leave Cindy out of it for now.

Novaterra tried to provide kids to administer themselves for speciality, if they were mentally well-endowed. They had the right to change their minds at any time during the course of growing up. As they got older, many children fell into the jobs they had done, and they had a job for life. That was our way on Novaterra. That was the way of War. Everyone did their part, and children were no exception.

With Cindy, she didn't see anything wrong with putting blocks in particular patterns. She also didn't see anything wrong with being ahead of herself. But we did. *It was all in the mind.* Thia and I were astounded to learn of her 'techniques' and thought to seek professional advice about it.

One day, we took Cindy to a specialist who deals with spectrum disorders. We didn't know what it was of course, but we guessed it was a mental issue we were dealing with. At least if we were wrong, we could go elsewhere.

But we weren't wrong. And we went to the correct facility.

It was Asperger's.

I was told long ago that an ancestor Sucyn Shonnen had this condition. Even the infamous Cynthia Lear had it. God, I was shell shocked. It was hard enough to come to grips with preening fatherhood, but to have a child with a spectrum disorder was no mean feat.

'There's not anything you can do really,' Dr Salmuck replied, 'All she needs is tender loving care, and to allow for the quirky behaviours to develop, or die off. She may outgrow some things, but not others, and pick up on new things. Yet, they're not untenable. It isn't as if you had to keep her bound to you all your life. She can have a life; so, let it develop. Let her choose her life. All you can do is sit back, and look after her as best as you can.'

We walked out of the office stunned.

I moaned loudly, 'Why does this shit have to be inherited???!!!'

'At least she can live with it,' Thia commented. 'She may be a genius. I've read that people with Asperger's have very fruitful lives indeed.'

'More like fruity,' I sneered.

'Ah, love comes in all sorts. *It is how she is treated now that makes the difference*,' she said.

Cindy didn't say anything and just sucked on her finger.

'Well, I'm not planning to treat her like some psycho like Lear was. That is what got us into this mess in the first place,' I hurled.

'She'll be alright,' Thia said. 'Won't you be darling?'

Cindy looked from her buggy smiling and cooing, 'I'm fine, Mummy.'

'It didn't take much to read her, though,' I commented.

'She's like an open book,' Thia went on, *'It's what you read out of it that counts.'*

We walked ahead. Life didn't forebode anything. I kept thinking about little Cindy and how she'll get on. I guess I should listen to the wife and forget about how bad the condition was. It looked like we must concentrate on how good she will be later.

So, I suggested, 'How about lunch at your old commissary before we go back to base?'

'Yeah, let's away then,' she accepted.

We had our lunch and no one mentioned Thia being at the commissary. All her old workmates were busy doing other things.

Someone did remember her, but at closer glance, it turned out to be a recent addition. Guess going job to job had its spells.

When we returned to base, Private Jarris went up to me. 'How did it go?'

'How did what go? Lunch?'

'No, your doctor appointment. I overheard,' he said.

Unflinching, and oddly-caring, I stated, 'She's got Asperger's. It's a hereditary spectrum disorder. I've got it in my family.'

'Oh, I'm most sorry to hear that. At least she can live with it. Not like other disorders,' Jarris nodded.

He went up to Cindy and tousled her hair a bit. 'How's the little princess today?'

'Fine,' she said glumly, trying to be more grown up. A sign of the condition, so I heard from my predecessors.

Jarris gave me a big compliment. 'Well, that is one fine keen kindred you have, Daye.'

'Time will tell,' Thia interrupted, 'Baby, it's time for your nap. Let's go.'

'Awh, and I wanted to talk to the nice man here,' Cindy cried bitterly.

'You will have plenty of conversations when you are older, but now it is time for dozies,' Thia asserted herself.

'Okay, Mummy.' She backed down, but looked at Jarris intensely.

Thia took the chair, with Cindy still in it, into the other room, where she put the child down for a nap in the little cot. It will be fun putting her to proper sleep when she gets older.

Thia returned and apologised to Jarris. 'I'm so sorry Cindy acted that way. She's a nice girl, but just a little, ummm...'

Jarris considered, 'Quirky?'

'Yes. That's it. Quirky. She's got loads of it about.'

The private carried on. 'I think it may win her some wars in her day, don't you think?'

'Eh, maybe, but don't count on it. Nice to see you Jarris.'

Thia went back into the room with Cindy, leaving me alone with the man.

'Dexx wants you again,' Jarris said, 'I hope your little one will improve with time.'

'She will,' I skipped off to see the CO, 'I'll make sure of it.'

I went to the office where Dexx and an underling stood by.

'Dismissed,' he ordered, as the other entity left the room. 'Daye.'

'Yes, sir,' I saluted.

'At ease, soldier,' Dexx continued, 'You know you've got a wild one on your hands. I heard you talking to Jarris.'

I couldn't think of anything else to say, but I stated the obvious. 'Yes, sir!'

'I know I know. She's not going to turn out bad. You can't predict it, though. It's like a fighting soldier. You can train him into his gosh-darn misery. Doesn't mean he'll perform, or worse, he may choose to leave the military. Can't take it. You know what I mean. Parenthood, like soldiering, is how you make it.'

My face flushed with sadness and I wanted to cry very badly. But I didn't because I was in front of... DEXX.

'Anyway,' Dexx rifled through some papers, 'I've got another mission. Now, you don't have to do it, but I wouldn't be asking you if I didn't think you couldn't do it. In fact, I know you can and I know you will.'

'What is it, sir?'

'You and five other fighters will go out behind enemy lines and disable their loading generator. It is a small outfit; a small asteroid for you and yours to blow up, to prevent those aliens using that firepower against us. You have limited time and space to do it at, so you'll have to move in quick to get the job done. It is lightly manned, so you'd be lucky in that sense. But, don't take anything for granted, Daye, because those aliens will sniff you out like a shark and come after you with firepower that will overwhelm and disable *you*. I can't have that, and I can't have a yellow skin on the team. Will you do it, Daye?'

'I won't let you down, sir,' I stated with confidence.

'I hope so, and there is some danger to it, but I wouldn't have asked you if I didn't think you could do it. I have confidence in you and you're leading the team.'

I was crestfallen to think that he would put me in such a situation. I now had a child in need.

Yet, as if to read my mind, Dexx said, 'Don't worry if you don't come back. We'll look after Thia and Cindy.'

I was shocked to hear such a thing from the CO, but I extended my hand anyway in gratefulness, 'Thank you.'

We shook on it, and I saluted him again before leaving. I was to have a day to prepare for the journey.

CHAPTER IX

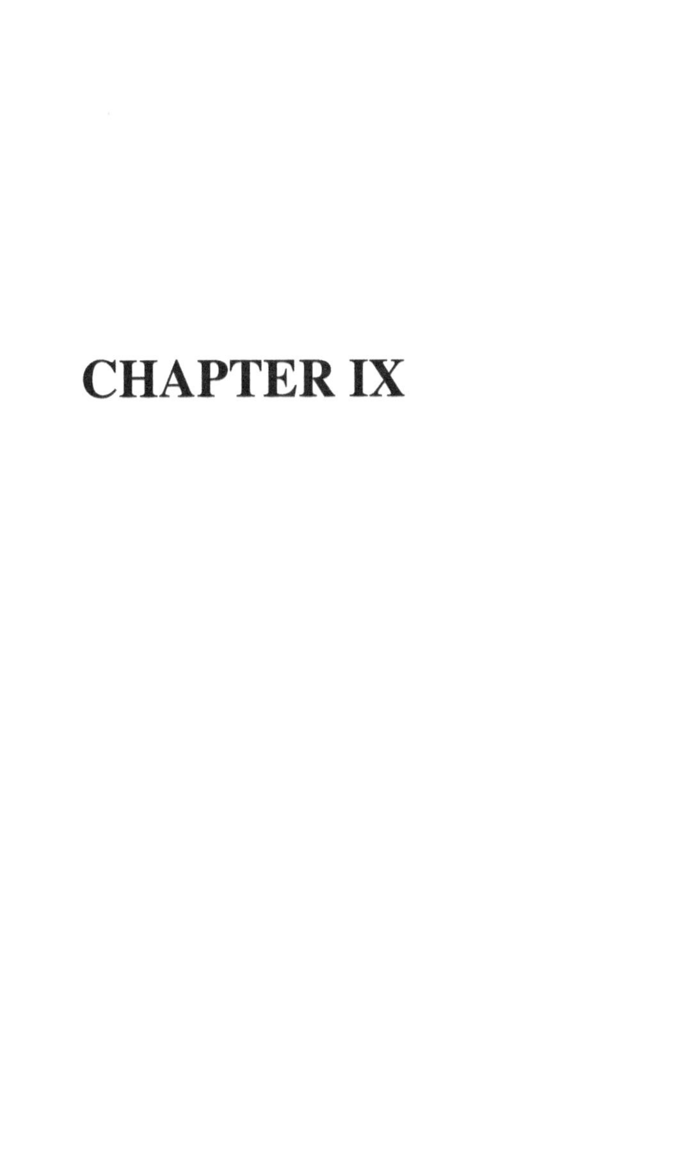

Meantime, the aliens were getting worse, and the need to knock out a mere generator was heightened at every second. They liked to bomb things, human targets especially, as that was the most pleasing act of the War for them. They were even worse when they raided. Sometimes, they would show themselves as the masters, and we, as a minor subspecies to them. Other times, it was just fly-bys, and mass destruction with them. They were relentless, scathing, and needed to be stopped.

But how? I could only do so much; any other ones in my division can only do so much. Civilians were grounded forever, unless for travel, and us military folk went straight up into space and get blasted like the stars they were. It was awful, and more difficult for me when I had to tell Thia about it. I had much to think about that night. There was much to tell about myself that I had not mentioned to anyone. We just didn't have the time. With the addition of Cindy's problem, everything now was left behind.

On my final night before the fateful mission, I decided to have a chat with Thia and let her know what's been missing. There wasn't much, though, but there was something I had to bring up with her. It would not be easy, but it would be worse for her and the child if things didn't work out, either.

In total calmness, I played my hand and dealt Thia some news about me. 'I've a twin brother in Sydmouth.'

'You never spoke of him. What's his name?'

'Elliott Michael Daye,' I revealed, 'He's just like me, but an accident rendered him impotent. He has no family but me.'

Thia felt sympathetic. 'I'm sorry Phil.' She gave me a hug.

'Maybe I should have mentioned him long ago.'

'I guess you're telling me about him, in case anything happens to you?'

'Yes. It's in my file anyway, but it is not something I would talk about. We were close, but grew apart over time. They don't make a big to-do about family unless for good reason.'

Thia sighed. 'Will we meet him?'

'I don't know. I don't know anything. I thought you should know before my mission.'

'Thank you,' Thia kissed me.

We hugged some more before little Cindy came into the room. 'I overheard what you said. 'What accident was Elli in?'

I smiled at her and put her on my lap.

I then thought about our early youth and the bitterness I endured since learning he was stuck in a ditch and I could not do anything, but run. Alien attacks were rampant, and it was lucky a human helped Elliott. The problem was it was the last I saw of him.

'Well Cindy,' I held the young child in my arms. 'It's like this...'

I told her and Thia about when our place got raided and bombarded by the aliens.

'Elliott and I had been outside playing, when an alien ship flew by, and doused our home with fire and burned it out. Dad was at home, on leave at the time; there was nothing we could do. When we turned around, there was nothing left.

'Elliott had dropped a ball or something, and he went back, when another bomb hit the house next to ours. It blew up, with Elliott getting thrown clear into a ditch. As I ran to get help, I was scooped up by a human patrol guard, who commended my intention but drowned me out. They would pick up Elliott later, they said.

'And they did. But his condition was so critical and they had to ship him to Sydmouth, where the hospitals there were more specialized. I don't know what happened to him after that. I was given word that he was okay, needing observation, but that was all I got. I later found out he was injured where it counted.' I pointed to my nether-bits. 'He later got over the injury and works from home, I heard. He was awarded compensation for his loss, but he will never have children. That is a horror because the human race cannot be overshadowed by these thieving bugs!'

Cindy was asleep by now, and as Thia put her to bed, she asked, 'Should we contact him? I mean it would be the best thing to do after all this time.'

'I agree with you, Thia, but I'll let the CO do that. You sit in comfort with me. I don't know how this mission is, but it sounds simple. I just have to knock out a generator on an asteroid or something, but there's a chance I might not see you again.'

'I hope for the best in your mission,' Thia smiled and gave me a kiss.

She remained with me through the night. A television show was on that brought back memories for me. It was about a twentieth-century place, somewhere in New England. I used to watch it when I was younger, and the fellow that played one of the characters looked a bit like me.

It did not go unnoticed by Thia, either. 'There's that guy who looks like you, Phil.'

'Yes, I know, honey. I know.'

I smiled ruefully, and gave Thia more love. It was all fiction then and nothing could blank out what time we had left together. I really wanted to have more time with her, to talk, to sleep, to play, even to work. I loved her all the more, and the more I thought of tomorrow, the more I wanted it to be today. The show carried on. We watched it in all its black and white glory. I kissed Thia in coloured glory.

When the show concluded, we fell asleep, arm in arm, hoping it will last forever.

CHAPTER X

The next morning, I flew out early with my team. They were just comrades-in-arms and would refer to them as such. Friendships here were not mandatory due to your lifespan. Any minute you could be snuffed out, and keeping tabs of your friends at this stage of the game proved too intensive. So, I stayed away from it. Yet, I did not smirk at marriage, which I did not regret. I was proud to be a husband and father. I was happy to bear such a joyful child as Cindy, despite her mental condition.

Before I left, I went up to the sleeping bears of Thia and Cindy, to give them kisses. To Thia, I gave her more, but eventually left them to their own devices. They'd be handling enough when I return... IF I return. There was no course nor reason to say anything, or even talk to them. I would rather my goodbyes be simple, but effective.

Thia woke up anyway, and caught me sneaking out.

'Phil?'

I stopped in my tracks. 'Thia, no...'

'Phil, I...,' she ran to me to give me a final hug. I hoped to give her more later on.

'Thia, I have to go,' I stated firmly.

'I know, but,' she looked at me with her big, bright, brown eyes. 'I wanted you to know we're praying for you and we love you very much.'

'Darling, I love you too.' I stayed with her for a few more moments.

God, it was difficult. Why did I have to go on *this* mission? Couldn't I just have stayed with Thia for another short time?

'I've got to go now, my love. If I'm not back, here is Elliott's number.' I reached in a drawer, and pulled out the number; I kept it just in case, all this time. I changed my mind about getting Dexx involved. 'You call him. He'll take care of you two,' I ordered.

Thia did not like being ordered, but this time, she felt the deep burden I carried. 'Okay, Phil. I'll contact him. I'll be waiting for YOU, though.'

'Don't wait too long, my love. If I'm declared dead, then phone him, got it?'

'Yes,' she cried.

With one more hug, I left the room. Thia was distraught, fretted, and anxious. She didn't even wake Cindy up. She couldn't. It was too much to bear. The note with Elliott's number stayed in her hand, then it went into her pocket.

After leaving her, I went to Dexx's office, where he gave the assembled pilots instructions for the mission, though I knew them already. I got it from the boss himself, alone. Once all was done, I blasted outta there with my thrusters on high, right into the stars. When we got that generator on the asteroid Zeta V destroyed, all would be well for the time being.

It didn't seem that difficult, but to get there, we had to bypass alien patrol ships and floating wastrels in the skies that they may throw at us. We didn't get far when I received a message from one of the other pilots.

It said, 'Alien ships on one-two port, alien ships on one-two port. Daye, do you read?'

'Loud and clear, 'I called out from my cockpit mike.

I shot the enemy ships at point-blank range. They disintegrated nicely, as I piloted my ship toward Zeta V. However, another raid was upon us, and a couple of our ships were taken out. There were four of us left. We hardly begun to reach our target.

To the others, I cried, 'Keep fighting, and shooting. Try not to play target practice from the ball's view, please!'

'Roger that,' said one.

'Okay boss,' called the other.

The third one clouded up in smoke and blew up from alien fire. Now, we were three.

I shouted, 'Damn guys, hold yourselves together!'

No response. *I guess that's due to them finding the asteroid... or...*

Another tail shot. Another one down.

'It's up to us now, Rae,' I said, 'Let's get to Zeta V.'

'Copy,' she said.

We raced to find the asteroid, and shot up aliens while doing so.

It wasn't far, but with enemy ships enclosing, Dexx was correct in what he said about the mission being dangerous and difficult. Zeta V was finally spotted, with its antenna and bulking barges housing wiry samples for our destruction. Well, it will be *their* destruction.

'Come on, Rae, I found what we're looking for,' I called out.

'Got it.'

'I'll make the run,' I continued, 'Cover me.'

'Okay boss.'

Rae stayed with me the whole time. She shot at alien ships, as I desperately tried to outrun them. They were Saturninon, which were the most ruthless and deadly. It was no wonder we lost much of our team to them.

I was getting closer to the generator, and scanned the outlying area. A blip on my screen informed me of it, and with all my might, I gave it enough of my firepower to rupture the generator, and it exploded. I was most happy and informed Rae of it...

... no answer.

Um... she was here just a minute ago.

I saw an outburst from a power magazine that blew up too, and Rae's now damaged ship was caught in the middle. She broke rank and tried to pull herself out of it. She jetted away from the alien trajectory, but they were too fast for her, and killed her outright.

I sat in silence, for a second, before I headed out of there post haste. I blasted my way past many alien ships, while crying out for company... *any company will do!* I travelled this far out into free space, when I saw more alien ships on my scanner, ready to belt me one. I thought I was out of the woods, when...

... a blast caved into my ship and I knew it was all over. I did what I had to do, even if I had to die doing it. At least humanity was safe, for now. I knew I gave a decent fight, and who knew where I would be next time...

... at least Elliott Michael Daye will have a better chance at it than me.

CYNTHIA DAYE

CHAPTER XI

It was hours, if not a day until we heard back about Daddy. A grim-looking man, probably in charge of the base, came up to Mother to tell her the news.

'Now, Mrs Daye,' the man began to say, 'I know it hasn't been long since he left, but...'

She shouted, 'He's dead, Dexx, isn't he?'

'Yes, he is.'

Mother looked at me fondly, and remembered that paper Daddy slipped to her earlier.

She had harsh words for Dexx, though. 'You shouldn't have sent him out there, with those murderous aliens!'

'I felt I did what I had to do. Would you want this base to be destroyed? Huh? There was a quick shot at an alien generator, and Daye had done it! At least you and your daughter are alive. We're not meant to grow old gracefully these days, are we?'

'Phil,' her tears were embittered, 'Why??'

'Mama,' I said, feeling left out.

She crossed a few barriers to get at me, and I don't mean literal ones.

'We'll have to go live with your Uncle Elliott,' she said.

'I have his number,' Dexx volunteered.

'So do I,' Thia answered, 'Thank you.'

'We have no time for a funeral,' he went on, 'All my pilots were lost.'

She cried, 'All of them?'

'Yes,' he said, glumly, 'All of them. At least we still have a base. Your husband fulfilled his task. Now, you contact your relative. I've got to get back to duty.'

'Duty, it's always duty,' she shouted.

Dexx ignored her grievances. He understood, but with a base to run, he couldn't afford to be cuddly with anyone. He left us to pick up the pieces and renew our family, even if it was with a relative.

We went back to family quarters, and I just sat there with my mouth to a small plush toy. Mother took the news rather hard, and took it out on the phone. Then she called the number on the paper.

'Elliott?'

'Yes, it's me. Who is this?'

'Thia Daye. I'm Phil's wife, at Lynchner Barracks. Could you come by, we need to talk.'

'Sure thing, Mrs Daye, ummm... how's Phil?

'Can we talk?'

'I'll come by.'

She hung up. It wouldn't be long, an hour or so on the hover car, depending how many miles he needed to take from Sydmouth.

'Baby, you need to pack your things,' she said to me.

'I don't have much, but all right.'

I gathered whatever clothing that fit me and toys that I was personally attached to. Everything else got donated to the base. There would be more children in future, and there was always a little body to clothe. Mother gathered hers and Daddy's things too.

An hour passed. I saw it on the clock, when a familiar face came in...

... and I screamed, 'DADDY!'

'Whoa, whoa there little girl,' Elliott said. 'I'm your uncle, Elliott. So, this is the illustrious Cynthia I've heard about.'

The shock pattered through me like rain. 'You're not Daddy?'

'Nope, just Elliott. I hope we can be friends, nay, family together.'

The earlier news about Daddy filtered through me, finally. 'Daddy's gone.'

'Yes, he is, but I'm here, and I will take care of you and your mother,' Elliott pulled himself together, upon hearing the news.

Mother walked in the room, 'Hi, Elliott.'

'Phil?'

'He's gone,' she said.

A pause of reflection passed. 'You're Thia Daye,' he whispered, thinking about his brother. 'I'm sorry. I lost him too, a long time ago.'

'I know, Elliott.' Mother gave him a hug, 'He told me everything the night before.'

'He knew he wasn't coming back, did he?'

'Just precaution, I guess,' Mother sighed.

Elliott went on. 'Well, let me have a look at you. My, my, what taste my brother had.'

'And what a looker you are too,' she said.

Elliott mused, 'Ha! I'm no better than anybody else. I cannot have children.'

Mother held onto me. 'You've got one here; the all-in-one, introverted kookiness,' Mother stated, showing me off to him.

He laughed, then said, 'Let's go, I'm itching to get back to Sydmouth. When we get there, we can eat something too. Would you like that?'

He crouched down to my level to kiss me. I gave him a hug.

'You look like Daddy,' I raved on still.

'I do, but I'm not,' Elliott told me. 'I do want to be a father to you somehow.'

'Can I call you Elli? Daddy is for Daddy,' I reckoned.

'Elli is fine, sweetness. At least for now.'

I screamed loudly for keeps, 'Forever!'

'Okay, okay,' Elliott sighed, taking our bags out.

'YAY!' I jumped into his arms, ignoring the baggage.

'I'll go say goodbye to the CO,' Thia said, 'Shan't be a moment.'

Elli waved to Mother, as he gathered me in his arms, with our baggage.

'Your mother is a good woman, little miss. I wouldn't want to miss out on her,' he said quietly.

'I love her, and Daddy too, wherever he is.'

'I'm sure he loves you still, wherever he is.'

Thia came out with Dexx.

'It's nice to finally meet you, Mr Daye. Phil was a fine pilot.' Dexx shook Elli's hand.

'I say he was, but I wouldn't have noticed,' he replied.

To me, Dexx commanded in a playful tone, 'And you, young lady, you kick some alien butt for your father, y'hear now?'

'Will do. Maybe you'll still be the commander,' I thought aloud.

Dexx roughly smiled, under a ten o'clock shadow. 'I hope so. You take care.'

With love and farewells, we left the base for good. Elliott had a small vehicle, which transported everything to his place in Sydmouth. A new piece of my life formed in front of me. No aliens attacked us, as the paths remained clear. I guessed everything was set against Daddy; that's why he's gone.

I thought about Elli and his resemblance to Daddy. I heard he was a twin, but I didn't understand it. I was only little and I didn't know of the wider spectrum like grownups did. I tried to accept Elliott as the new 'daddy', but I knew he would never be my father.

After an eternity in traffic, and migrating among other hover cars and non-entities, we finally made it to Sydmouth. Elli's place wasn't far and there were quite a few shops around, where we could go out for a bite, and to have a look around. I didn't care about the shops right now. I just wanted to go 'home', wherever that was.

It wasn't a large family house on Malone Drive. Probably a one or two bedroom place. It didn't look big to me, but when we got inside, the space was enormous. I wondered why Elli didn't have a family of his own, but it didn't concern me. We were his now!

'Make yourselves comfortable. I've got an extra bedroom for Cynthia,' he offered.

I asked, 'Elli?'

'Yes,' he answered.

'Can you call me Cindy. Everyone else does.'

'Sure, Cindy.'

I gave him an even bigger hug, and he scooped me in his arms and took me to the other bedroom. It had a bed, dresser-drawer set, a mirror, and a window with a small seat beneath.

'Now, this can be your room. I know it's not much, but you can fill it in with fun things,' he said. 'You can pick out stuff in the shops that's special to you.'

'Daddy, Daddy's special to me,' I cried.

'Well I can't take back what life dealt ya, honey. I know you lost him, but I am going to endeavour to be the best father to you. And I promise it.'

He crossed his heart and I decided to hold him a little longer. He may not be 'daddy', but I was willing to go along, and let him be a more special father-like entity.

We got cosy as a family together. My new room was set up nicely and ready to go. I know it didn't have much, but I didn't have much to begin with. Mother moved in with Elli, and started unpacking. Thankfully, I didn't have much to unpack. I only had a small suitcase, filled with a few outfits, a couple of toys, but nothing much else. The main bulk of toys were left on the base, as I outgrew them, and new children would come along to play with them instead. With all the places to go round here, I take it I will be spoilt for choice.

CHAPTER XII

We all settled into our new lives at Sydmouth. I began to go to nursery school, kindergarten, and later on, grade school. Mother and Elli settled down too, even more so, when they decided to get married. It was a prudent move, but it was not a bad one. We were already a family with one kid, so why not?

There was a nearby church, Bywinster Central, where it took place. It wasn't a fun ceremony, but it was needed to cement our lives together. They married when I was five. Elli was now the new 'daddy', but due to the agreement we made when I first met him, he allowed me to still call him Elli. It wasn't much, a few friends of Elli's were present, and the minister. They exchanged vows and promised to be faithful and love each other to death. My problem was, how could you love someone to death? Wouldn't that be rather cruel?

I don't remember alot at this time. Going to the park, going shopping, going to school, and the doctor, too. It wasn't much. Other children played in parks, at school, but I never bothered with them much. Some of them took interest in me, and I tried to play on occasion, but it was fleeting, then everyone had to go home. My life was frustrating that way. If it wasn't for school or parks, where would people my age go to play?

My condition also became more pronounced as I got older. Medical notes were shifted from Lynchner to Sydmouth and the doctors had a fun day looking, I bet! The notes told a whopping tale about me. I recall only hearing stuff like, 'she'll be fine; just give her love and plenty of attention.' It felt like all the time in the world. Attention was all I had. No one else was around to cater to. I was an only child and was treated as such.

I wondered about the War and why Daddy was really gone. Mother and Elli didn't mince words with me about it. Would aliens really take away life?

My family tried to be honest with me. In telling me later about someone named Lear who started this obstruction, I felt horrified that it was just someone like me, with the same condition! But it was someone like me who was treated very poorly. Badly. Abominably. No love, no affection, no attention. Just bad, bad, bad, bad! How can anyone live like that????! Secretly, I thought if I had that option, I would go to the alien's cause as well, and strike humanity down before it overturns us all!

I still wanted the War to end. I kept asking when it will end.

'Not now, Cindy,' was the usual answer to that one.

Life was temperate in Sydmouth. I grew and grew. The schools I went to were mediocre. Not that they were bad, but they weren't great either. Sometimes I missed my Daddy; so I thought to give Elli extra hugs, to allow for Daddy's spirit to embrace him, hoping I would get him back.

When I withdrew, the plan didn't work.

'It's just me, sweetness,' Elli said.

I sighed and wandered through the troughs of my mind to find what other garbage the demons would bring me. Being a teen didn't speak much to me either. I took the era in stride and attempted good when I tried not to fail. No boy-stuff either. I wasn't really prepared for that. Ugh! I didn't want to feel like I had to pander down to their expectations. It wasn't easy, nor lenient, I could tell you.

I stayed often in my room, either reading, doing homework, or watching television. There wasn't much to do. I got together with a school friend or two, but it wasn't much. Just a jolly day out. Or a day in. Take your pick.

There wasn't much doing to take the edge off the War. A great many were scared of capture by the enemy. I was sure as much glad I wasn't a bug...

... but Mother confessed otherwise to me, one day.

'I was raised as one, but I'm really a human-Silardian. I took a DNA test to prove it,' she stated.

That was all she said about it, and I left that rocket science behind. I sallied forth into the spacious room where Elli was. He was reading a newspaper in his rocker. There was a sofa I sat on, next to the rocker.

I asked him, 'Life's prospects aren't interesting, are they?'

He stopped reading, and stared at me. 'What makes you say such a thing like that?'

'I dunno, I just think it'll end some day.'

'Yes, my dear, it will,' he assured me, 'But not now. It does not have to end if you don't want it to. There will be opportunities, when all this is over, things will get back to normal. You'll see.'

'I guess,' I crossed my arms, looking dumpily at him.

'Look, I can't give you what I'm not entitled to. You've got a good home, good education, decent food, and people to love. If it's school you're worried about, pay it no mind. It's the real world that counts.'

He was right. I sloshed and sighed, walking to the edge of the doorframe, where I saw a fantastic sunset. I wanted to be part of it. I wanted to see more of it. I ran out the door, down the stairs, and into the garden.

Elli, meanwhile, went back to his newspaper.

What a boring fuck! I bet Daddy would relish this entitlement. Entitlement, indeed! Who did he think he is, this Elli?? All he does is read a newspaper, and I am looking at a sunset.

But my weakness was I didn't wanna be alone. It wasn't a grave fear, but I didn't like it...

...so ...

I screamed, 'Elli!'

Without thinking, he jumped from the rocker, and ran out the door to me.

'What is it, honey?'

I looked at him in shade. 'I wanted you to share this sunset with me.'

'Ohh, you little,' he gathered me up, 'Come here, princess.'

We kissed, but not that way. That way was for Mother.

And I ain't a mother, yet.

CHAPTER XIII

It was a few years later, and I was about to turn eighteen. School came and went and college was on the horizon. But so were the alien attacks. I felt I had to do something for the cause. I was rolling in emotional turmoil, when I looked at Elli, sure fast and steady. He made a good surrogate father to me; that I was grateful for. But. He seemed to be more than that. Mother got all the experience of loving, even though nothing would come of it. It must have been pretty relieving to go to the watering hole, without fear or contemplation...

... 'you're pregnant!'

It was a scarce resource, pregnancy. I certainly didn't allow guys to fool around with me. I secretly wanted to save that for another time, maybe with... nah, that could never be. How can I give myself when there was someone around, playing 'father' to you and you do not know what to do with yourself???? Despite Elli's disability in no longer providing more children, I thought he did alright. Mother loved him and I did too. Not in that way. Ever. Yet, he looked rather... rather... fetching. He had a slight tan about him, with greying hair, though full on all sides. A real man's man, I thought. The grey covered some brown that peeped out on some corners, but not many. I wondered what it was like, going grey at all corners. Sheesh! It must be scary to think.

Mother took care of me, walking me to school, feeding, helping with homework, and being a housewife. Her food skills were obvious and I was thankful for her Silardian heritage, because they were the best trained cooks in the galaxy. Recently, she'd been delving into Irish cooking and the dinners we had were immaculate. It took me to a faraway land, and Elli (who was Irish), to a place of strange ancestors; a place where he wished he could thrive in, maybe meeting that Muffyhuer Conna character he was descended from.

I guess this ancestor was no different from you and me, or even Elli. I even heard there was a woman called Cindihan, and she had a small resemblance to Mother. Could there be a connection? I was told I was named for her, so I wondered.

Elli still worked from home, and he did quite well in his consulting. I did not know what. I needed consulting of my own... from him! It drove me crazy thinking about boys, and men. It was horrible, not being able to express those feelings. I wanted so badly to go up to Elli and confess my heart out to him, but I couldn't and I wouldn't. So enough said. I took the blame for my own self-pardon, though I find it frustrating as heck!

Eventually, I was allowed to go off on my own. I went on the hover cars to school, one by one, back and forth; to friend's houses also. Yet friends still didn't come easy for me. They were more acquaintance-like than real friends, mostly due to the Asperger's holding back my social skills. Of course, on a clearer day, you would ask, 'what social skills?' That is what I thought of the whole mess. I didn't mean to be so harsh about it, but when you're fighting the enemy, looking out for aliens, and 'not who's coming to see you tonight', you'd get a pretty sore head over it.

Life continued at a drab pace. No sparkle of invasion yet, but no word from the aliens, either. Where would they strike next? They would strike out at someone, somewhere; who was the question. Other parts of Novaterra got ransacked. The eastern hemisphere of the planet was blasted, all in front of us on our television monitors. There were multitudes of trees that were destroyed and a once-lively forest was gone. We needed those trees to fell and grow back. Now, there was nothing, because the aliens took the trees for their own purpose. Like us, they didn't waste convenient resources either.

They tried to bomb out cities. Back and forth, back and forth. The drudgery of it was sickening, but we were ready for them. Pilots were drawn from all bases on Novaterra to strike out at the aliens. They picked them off like cobwebs (that they were), and luckily nothing significant was destroyed in the process.

Soon, my eighteenth birthday arrived. June 12, 3187. Okay, so it was just a number on a calendar. So what? It was MY number on the calendar! That morning, Elli came up to me and gave me a kiss.

'Happy Birthday, sweetness,' he cooed in my ear. 'I bought this for you.'

He handed me a small wrapped case. What could it be? A ring, I betcha!

'It's for you to remember me by,' he said, as I viciously opened it.

I was right, it was a ring.

'Thanks, Elli,' I gave him a hug. It was a golden band, with an emerald in the middle. Funny, it looked like an engagement ring to me!

Mother came in the room with a gift in her hand. 'Congratulations, Cindy. Here's my gift to you.'

I opened that one a bit more carefully, as it too was small, and I didn't want to seem eager.

Well, well, what do you know? It was a brooch. A clasp, cross shaped, golden like the ring, and small. I put it on my upper right hand chest area above my heart.

'I'll always remember you for this,' I smiled, hugging her, 'Thank you.'

Elli was eager to eat. 'Right, now who's for cake?'

He brought us into the kitchen to show off a mean looking spread. Finger food, sweetmeats, drinks, and THE cake were all on display. I marvelled at it, and we all tucked in. The food was made by Mother; surprise, surprise! It was laid out by Elli. Sometimes, I'd look at him and wonder what Daddy would do on such an occasion. Probably the same, I reasoned to myself.

When it was time to cut the cake, I breathed loudly to blow out the candles, hopefully with one breath.

'Magnificent,' Elli shouted in gladness, as he got a sharp knife out to cut the cake.

'That took much out of me,' I exhaled sharply.

'Well, you're young yet. Wait 'til it's MY birthday, then we'll see who gets in first,' he commented.

I smiled, laughed and ate the cake. White chocolate icing with an apple fruit filling. It was good.

Out of a jokey nature, I asked, 'Who made this?'

'Your mother,' came Elli's quick-laced reply.

'Figures,' I smiled at her.

Mother smiled back. She was unsure of my status in life and wanted to talk to me further.

She asked me, 'What do you plan to do when school's over?'

'I don't know,' I replied. 'Maybe help out the Cause.'

'They're looking for workers,' Elli went to a newspaper. 'Here it is.'

I read the advert. *'Looking for adventure, or at least work? Come down to the recycling plant to sort out materials for weapons refurbishment. Call Wolfe-Harris, at...'*

I interjected, 'You want me to work at a recycling plant?'

'Sure, lots of young people are doing it,' Elli enthused. 'And as you're not at the moment, college-bound, I think it would make a good start for you.'

'True,' I sighed, 'I'll wait until school finishes, and...'

'You get your name there now, young lady,' Elli insisted, 'They could be filled up in a few weeks time. They're looking now.'

'Elli,' Mother said, 'Don't pressure the lass.'

'Look, you have a bit of time to think about it, but I would go for it, even if you are still in school. You'll finish up in a few weeks, and the following Monday or so, you could be at your first job!'

I thought about it and wondered about Elli's eagerness to get me working. Was it that his firm wasn't paying him near enough?

'Okay, Elli, I'll go after school, see what's doing,' I caved in.

'Good,' he gave me a kiss on the head. 'You won't regret it. And the money will come in useful. You'll be a working girl, my lass!'

A working girl... I mused at the title. Sounded steamy, but if Elli felt it was a necessity, then I went along with it.

CHAPTER XIV

The next day, I went to the plant after school, as I planned. I took the hover car out to where it was, Battlenook Way, on the docks of Sydmouth Shore. I felt pretty silly being fresh-faced and pitifully naive about going to a factory for work. When I arrived, the place was teeming with people, all doing the same thing. Sorting out materials. Recycling materials. What did they need me for? Yet, I thought about what Elli said, and decided to have a go at it.

I filled in an obligatory form, and waited for someone called Wolfe-Harris. Weird name. I wondered what his story was!

A kindly gentleman, middle-aged, with bags of character under his eyelids approached me. 'Are you, um, Cynthia Daye?'

'I am. You must be Mr Wolfe-Harris,' I replied, shaking his hand.

'Good. I trust you are still in school?'

'Yes. They let out in a couple of weeks or so, and I am finished, save for college.'

'What do you plan to do then?'

'Work, I suppose. I'm a fast learner, but I've got Asperger's.'

'You will have to be, in order to work here,' he said, wobbling on, taking me through the factory. 'Your condition has been noted, and it should not bear a fig on how you do for me. Come, I'll show you the insides.'

The main floor had masses of people going through mountains of trash to get at the sacred recyclable materials. Plastics, tins, glass, cardboard were all put in their place, and whisked away to become weaponry for our cause.

I interjected, 'This is all for the war effort?'

'Yep,' Wolfe-Harris stated, 'All of these scrap materials you find on the streets could become a cannon, or laser pistol or such not. All you need is to separate glass from plastic from tin, etc. They go in receptacles and the munitions people do the rest.'

'Could I work after school or weekends?'

'Perhaps. I think we can arrange it,' he smiled. 'When can you start?'

'I can start anytime,' I blurted out.

'Leave your details with my clerk up front and I will contact you shortly.'

'Many thanks, sir.'

'I look forward to seeing you soon.'

I went out of the factory and out the door. Mother, oddly enough, was waiting for me.

She asked, 'Hi, did you make it?'

'They said they would contact me,' I said.

'Fine. The money will come in handy. Want something?'

'Sure,' I walked alongside her. 'Where's Elli? I thought he would be with you.'

'He's waiting for us,' she grinned.

We went to a Silardian outpost and had a small meal there. As Mother would have it, Elli was waiting for us.

'I thought it would be a nice surprise if we all got together,' he stated.

'It is nice here,' Mother replied.

We sat at a table, had our orders taken and started chatting.

Elli began, 'So, you working yet, little bun?'

Thinking it was about me, cos Mother could not be called a 'little bun', despite her short stature, I answered, 'They'll contact me when they need me.'

'Alright.'

'They may ask me to work after school or on the weekend,' I added.

'Fine,' Elli shook his head.

The food arrived; we ate, paid, then went home in the small hover car.

'I wish you packets of good luck, if they take you on fully,' he said.

'Thanks,' I gave him a quick hug.'

* * * * * *

School ended rather abruptly, due to an alien attack on an adjacent street. Luckily, we took our final exams, and everybody did well.

Graduation ceremonies were put on hold indefinitely, as the school had offered to help clean up the street that got hit. Everyone pitched in like that. It was a hardworking ethic, but it proved that humans were not to be messed with lightly.

Meanwhile, I did start work at that recycling plant. It was hum-drum, and very boring, though. For a normal person. For me, I liked it, because its repetitiveness fitted into the profile of my condition of Asperger's. Spectrum disorders loved order, and this job I had was as orderly as it got! There wasn't much to it, really, but it was as important as being a pilot like Daddy was. I put on a small pinafore and gloves, and started sorting out all the waste Novaterra could muster.

And it could muster a lot, because humanity's waste will be its salvation.

I made some friends along the way too. There were plenty of people there that were friendly, for the most part. Those that weren't, just kept to themselves, and maybe muttered a 'hello'. I was paired with a fellow by the name of Zavv Longsearch Lynchner.

'You mean Lynchner Barracks?'

'My great-great-grandfather founded it,' he proudly stated.

'I'm Cindy. Cindy Daye.'

'Nice to meet you,' he went over to the largest pile of waste I'd ever seen. 'This is our lot. We have a few hours to get the gems out for munitions. Want to help?'

'Yeah,' I eagerly went for it.

'Hey, not so fast, girl!' He held my shoulders. 'Haste makes more waste. You don't want to do that. Take your time, just not too much.'

'Okay.' I began the sorting process.

'Why did you want to do this line of work?'

'I thought to help with the War, like Daddy.'

My countenance turned, and Zavv noticed it. 'Killed, I bet?'

'Yes.' I threw a soda bottle into a container. 'I have a stepfather though, and my mother still lives.'

'At least you have family. My brothers all work here, and have been for a few years. Well, they're not really brothers, but we've been close over these years. You said your name was Daye?'

'Yes, Cynthia Daye, but everyone calls me Cindy.'

'Daye,' he muttered. 'Daye. Conna Daye, by some chance?'

'I'd heard of Muffyhuer, if that's who you mean.'

'No, no,' Zavv threw a foil into its pile. 'Wait.' He tried to recall nearly two to three millennia of history... possibly his own!

I carried on chucking stuff into the bins, when I heard someone overhead, 'Hi Zavv!'

'Hi, Backnah,' Zavv called out. 'That's Backnah, one of my 'brothers', if you get my meaning.'

'Hi,' I waved.

Backnah waved back and dealt with his haulage.

Later on, Wolfe-Harris came by to see how I was doing.

'Fine, sir, I managed to get that large pile all sorted out,' I said.

'Nicely done,' he complimented. 'We'll get that to munitions. It is good to see you here, and on the double.'

'Yes, sir,' I saluted, tackling on another pile of scrap.

I realised the saluting reminded me of Daddy. Was I becoming him?

Lynchner saw me and was worried. 'You okay, girl? You look like you'd seen a ghost. Wolfe-Harris is far from that, you know.'

I exited out of the reverie post-haste. 'No, no, I'm okay. I just thought of Daddy for some odd reason. He used to be a pilot, but got killed in an alien attack. Or so it says.'

Zavv hugged me. 'It's alright. We'll give those aliens a run for their money, eh?'

I smiled and spent time with Zavv. He wasn't that much older, but nearly Daddy-age... maybe Elli-age. I didn't care. He seemed nice, with his fair skin, blue eyes, and he knew of this Muffyhuer fellow. I asked him about it.

'Yes, we are related. Muffyhuer's real name is Conna of Cobhayr, and I am descended from that lineage.'

'So you're a Daye?'

'Not exactly, but our roots are the same. That middle name of Longsearch gives it away, if you're looking for it. Thankfully, no one cares about that sort of thing anymore. We're all in it to survive, aren't we?'

I thought about it, as I spewed cans and bottles away into their containers. With such an outfit, I didn't think we'd ever lose. It was a crazy time, and I confess I enjoyed my being there. I looked forward to many years to come.

I went home later that evening, when Elli and Mother were at the table.

'You're late,' she said, 'We expected you a half-hour ago.'

'Sorry, I made some friends and we got chatting, you know,' I weakly replied. 'Traffic was pretty bad, too. There was another attack, and routes had to be changed. It was insane.'

'Okay,' Elli said, 'As long as you're here.'

He leaned over to kiss me.

'Not as insane as another alien attack,' Mother chided.

'You never know when,' Elli answered, passing the meat plate to me.

Their comments to me reverberated in my head for days.

CHAPTER XV

It hadn't been long since my working at the bottle plant on Battlenook Way. I liked it, and it was good for the Cause. It was good for us too, cos they paid pretty well, thinking it would be a life or death situation.

Elli was nearing his 60s by now and Mother hadn't worn out a bit at 50. She was lucky that way. Maybe I can be, too, but right now, I looked like a right fish. I was now nearing 19, and a lifetime ahead of me. I still looked like a teen, at times acted like one, due to the Asperger's. I couldn't help it, and there was much in my life that I could help either.

Every day at that Battlenook factory was the same. Not much going on, not many alien strikes. Just day after day, it seemed, it was just collecting bottles, but not on the street. There were people who did that, and put them in the waste bins around. Garbage was collected hourly, so as to get to those valuable resources. It was good to be surrounded by others who thought like you, somewhat. Mr Wolfe-Harris was good to us, and provided bonus pay, as well as other incentives, for getting the work done fast. You then get to live another day with a comfortable pay check.

My sight was fair, my uniform of smock and gloves were on, as I filed away my troubles. Not that I had much bother, really, but it was usual teen angst catching up with me. I didn't like that, cos I wanted to be better, but the Asperger's lets me down and I cannot help my actions.

And there was definitely one thing I couldn't help...

... Elliott Daye.

Though he wasn't my real father, he was a relative; an uncle, and my dad's twin brother. I still called him Elli so as not to confuse him with Daddy. He wasn't much to look at, if you just glanced at him (and you usually would do), there was more to him than I thought, from the beginning.

He was a looker. Nice, handsome, pretty blue eyes, slightly tanned skin, thin framed, and casually dressed. He could spiff up if need be, but most of the time, he'd be staying home working, so he just wears what he wants.

With gyros on the firing line, that I did not know what to do with, I had to think of something pretty fast to deal with this. Being a teenager was a rough business, and it got rougher as I aged. Being a full-blown adult, was even worse, especially if you were lonely. I never made many friends, give or take the one or two I had growing up. Boys were an enigma to me, men were even more so, but they were more desirable. I had friends at Battlenook, oh yes, but they were just that, friends. Man-friends, to be precise, but still a goodly platonic fellowship.

The problem was I wanted to board that ship and do stuff, but I daren't cos of their families, or were they married? I never asked. Never saw rings on fingers, either. You couldn't wear them in a bottle plant! To further my problem, I wasn't really interested in them in THAT regard. I just enjoyed talking, mixing, and throwing away bottles. That was my life, and that was all I aspired to be.

But...

One day, Mother had to go out shopping and called out, 'I'll return shortly. Look after Elliott for me, yeah?'

'Yes, Mother,' I called back.

'Look after Elliott for me'; who did she think she was?? Sheesh!

She called him by his full name in a normal sense. Yet, I am sure she has her secret 'pet' names for him, that they probably coo about in bed or something.

My jealous tinge got the better of me, and I made my way to the target. I can see the alien's point of view now. It made it easier to digest the War more fully. It made him easier to digest...

'Cindy, will you get me the remote? You don't mind, do you?'

It was him.

Yes, dear Elli, I DO mind, I thought.

I went to the holder and took it out, cradling it carefully.

'Alright,' I said, handing him the needed item.

'Thanks. Would you like to watch TV with me? Let's see what we have here,' he fumbled though his newspaper to the columns.

He checked the listings and found an old-Earth documentary about prehistoric history. Pre-hysteric, more like. I watched him, as he watched the program. I just stared and stared; he was into prehistory; I was getting into HIM! The feelings leapt into more salacious territory; not a crumb in sight. Everything was eaten, as I was...

Then came a raging question. Elli saw me flush red. 'You okay, Cindy dear?'

NO, I AM NOT OKAY!

But, I lied. 'Yes, I'm fine.'

'This here is good. It's nice that we can share something together.'

I wanted to scream. NO! I WANT YOU!

'It is nice to spend time with you. Not many things are spent together,' I stupidly replied.

He smiled and continued to watch the show. Goddammit! Why did I feel so (arrrrrrrgh!) about this?

A few more minutes passed by. The program went on to mention animal mating, and how it was done back in the day of the program, many years ago. It was probably no different between now and then, anyway. It was getting silly, but I was getting serious.

I then asked something rather dumb. 'Do ghostly waves have many hours?'

Elli's face was a-flash, like bright candy. 'WHAT?'

I laughed at him. He laughed back at me.

'You may be a dynamic man on the moon, but it is your moon to be dynamic on,' I carried on, sarcastically.

Elli was getting a message, but it was still in code. 'I'm going to chase you up that crippled creek, and lay there like a pillow for your beliefs.'

Now, I wasn't prepared for THAT in my code book!

We sat in silence, still, unaware that a raging emotion was surging.

'I'd rather have gone out with Mother, doing insignificant shopping,' I rattled on loudly.

Was Elli getting it?

I think he was.

So, he replied, brushing my fringe away from my eyes. 'Well, you're here with me, girl.'

He kissed me on the forehead.   That was all I needed to break away from the madness.

Our emotions were cast aside, including all hypnomas, dreads, taboos and the communal garden variety transfusion of 'we may not make it out alive'.

We did not care.   We kissed rather rampantly on the sofa.   The documentary was still on, but there was another program I wanted to watch. Him and me, starring, you guessed it, him and me!

'I don't know if we'll be alive again,' I cried.

'You know I can't have children, but I do work down there, somewhat,' he explained.

I felt totally unsure, but it was a moment not to be unmeasured. It was worse if you knew you would die in the next alien attack, and your feelings were not made clear.

Oh, I wanted my feelings to be quite clear. Sorry Mother.

Elli grabbed the remote, and switched the set off.

'Don't tell her,' he ordered.

'I won't,' I promised.

We rushed into a passionate frenzy, keeping that promise good and tight in the arboretum.

CHAPTER XVI

One of the aliens was having a very bad day. Legosu, son of Legolas, was itching to fight again, after a few days of boredom. He felt angry because his squadron wasn't picked for the previous mission. Damn. He wanted to get out there so badly, it hurt. It happens to bug things, don't it?

So, what to do? Lead another attack on Novaterra.

Legosu went to see the Commander, Prima, about it, to which he responded, 'Anywhere in particular?'

'Any ol' where; I don't care,' came the confident answer.

Prima checked a schedule on screen. 'Well, the 12th squadron is up today over Sydmouth. Does that put your hasty piles away?'

'Anything,' the alien Legosu thanked him, and went on his way.

He knew it could be a human defeat again. He understood this pilot's sanity, and carried on perusing his charts.

Legosu took his squadron into space, to meet the 12th and scanned the area with a ravishing pulsar, strapped to the back of his ship. It ravished, it raved, and craved delight in death, usually someone else's. The scanners had a very long range, so the ships couldn't be picked up by Novaterrans.

The pulsar picked up on a small blip on screen. Legosu examined closer, and tried to get a fix on the character. Who was she, he wondered, but upon even closer inspection, a blue light flashed in code and a message read out, 'Do not touch.' Why? He carried on, the paper mentioned it was Cynthia Daye, the descendant of the great Cynthia Lear. Oh, that's too close for me, he thought to himself, and put the pulsar away.

He flew the ship toward another point and carried on working. It was harrowing, due to a possibility that his flight path might be noticed.

There were people in the streets. Other people. Ah, that's better, Legosu sighed intensively. No Lear descendants here, just mucky humans. He thought about the girl that was on his scanner...Daye. He felt sorry for her, being a descendant of Lear, and living among these... these...! Legosu hadn't a word for them, he hated them so much. Still he shed a tear for the lass, knowing what was at stake here.

He waited for the signal to approach. The monitor blipped again, showing the coordinates for target areas, mostly in the Sydmouth region, just as the commander had said. The next thing Legosu saw was one of his combatants wing-diving into the street where he was silently monitoring. Gosh, these young ones were fast!

So he swung into action, ripping lasers on concrete like mini-pellets against a flimsy cardboard. He saw many of the enemy running away, trying to survive, but he fired his guns at them. He barraged street after street, seeing more fleeing coward-humans, taking refuge, wherever they could, trying to gain a speck of survival...

... but it was too late.

One of the larger alien ships gathered momentum, and bombed the vicinity, killing more venomous creatures below. Some of the alien ships went down too, in suicide runs, just to put their tuppence in. The devastation was clean, but brutal.

Ah well, another day, another human, Legosu thought as he continued his bombardment of Sydmouth.

He smiled, and took his device out of its holster on the board. 'Command quadrant, Command quadrant, TCP do you read?'

A crackle decoded itself on the speaker, 'Copy. What is your station?'

'The humans are dead or running. Buildings destroyed. Good chunk of Sydmouth in ruins. Anything else?'

'Let them take a run for their money. I'm sick of this war!'

Legosu cried out, 'Commander!'

'Just kidding, pilot. Report to base. You did all you could. We have others who will finish them.'

'Roger that.'

'Roger who?'

'Never mind, just an old-world joke.' Legosu switched off and returned to his base.

On the way, there was a waiting human force up in the air. Legions of star pilots of Novaterra's vast world came up to defend it. And it was worth defending, as a natural planet, a good pick and sustained life as they knew it. The best part was they also had practice training on their respective bases, Lynchner being one of them.

Legosu was intrigued but was caught off-guard. He did his bit for the Learian cause, but it seems the humans had the better end of the stick. Of course, it depended on where you picked up the stick in the first place.

'That'll teach you to mess with us,' cried a pilot, as his lasers fired on Legosu's ship, ending the alien's existence instantly.

More human pilots shot ships down faster than a bullet. Yet bullets weren't used anymore, so the speed of one would have been forgotten in this latter time, 32nd century era.

'There's no more filth,' another pilot commented, 'Let's get outta here.'

Another cried, 'We got them all!'

The human attackers went down to Novaterra in celebration.

* * * * * *

Meanwhile, during the attacks, I was with Wolfe-Harris in the basement of the Battlenook complex. It was most fortunate I made it to work, just as the bombings started. I was worried about my family, and how they managed. Did they manage? Now, I was among strangers, and good feelings for one another would be sorely tested.

'I tried to get as many workers out,' cried Wolfe-Harris, 'I don't think it was enough. I believe I tripped on some bodies.'

'What?' I shook my head. 'You did what you could do. At least I'm here.'

'Yes,' he hugged me, 'It's a refreshment to the mind you're safe.'

'We won't be safe for long,' I noticed the wall starting to buckle up.

'Let's get out of here; I'll check the damage outside.'

We left quickly, as that wall collapsed, and the basement was covered in rubble. Outside, it was no different, with people formerly with us, panicking and running, fleeing for their lives.

'I wonder how my folks are,' I said.

'Never mind your folks for now,' he rushed me, 'Let's go.'

We crept away from the factory to see the damage. The building was totalled, so we left just in time. There were bodies laying everywhere, sprawled all over.

'That could have been you,' he further said to me.

'I know.' I cried a bit, because I did not see anyone I knew, like Lynchner.

I inquired about that.

'He's dead, with all the others,' came the gruff answer.

We ran to another street, knowing our deal was done. There was no employment, no life, possibly no home...

... home.

So I asked him, 'Can we see if my family's okay?'

Wolfe-Harris looked at me. 'We will. Let's go to my place first.'

'Okay,' I droned, getting into his craft.

He took me and we flashed through street after street, with no let up. It wasn't far, though, and soon we were there. On Byrne and Davies Street. His eyes were peeled for more attacks from above.

'I don't think there are any more,' I quipped.

'Our pilots must have gotten to them first,' he replied.

'We would have seen more aliens by now, sir.'

'Yes Cindy. By the way, please call me Cedric. Makes it easier, yeah? Not so formal now.'

'Thanks,' I grinned at him.

I glanced at the name mentally. Cedric. Sounded very old fashioned, but I guess this fellow was, despite him living, when he was living. It felt like the future's past. I wondered how far I could go with the idea, but he was much older, even older than poor Lynchner.

We entered the building, but the insides were gutted. Cedric looked around, and couldn't find anything of value or such to take with him. All the early, nonsense ties of his life were destroyed in the bombings. He started to weep, and I stared out, in general.

'There's nothing here for me. We'll go to your place now,' he offered.

We went on the craft and sped to my place, which was...

... the entire block was gone.

Blown up out of proportion, gas-tanked away from here. Everything was gone. My stuff, the once-beautiful garden, my parents...

... my parents??!!

I hurried to find bodies, bodies to pin-point location.

They were there alright. Straight out of a scary movie. Mother was barely recognisable, but for the wedding band on her finger. Elli was, was...

I began to cry bitterly. Didn't we...?? Oh GOD! I bawled my head off.

Cedric was there to pick up any pieces worth picking up.

'There there,' he put me into his arms.

'But I just, saw him, we, we, we...,' I continued to stutter.

'I know, I know.'

I screamed inside, Know? You don't know, sir!!

I remained silent, and let the moment pass. I noticed my room was phased up; nothing was left of the place. I took Mother's wedding band, and anything else that may be valuable, including the ring that Elli gave me a year or so ago.

I then asked, 'Could we leave?'

'Don't you want to see them buried?'

I exhaled and started to whisper, when construction worker came up to us.

'You folks need to move on, we have rebuilding to do all over Sydmouth. The sooner we get on, the better.'

Another worker followed on, 'There's a homeless shelter down the road, and a hotel, if you're lucky.'

I desperately asked, 'Can we bury my parents?'

Cedric looked at me, 'Come on, Cindy.'

The workman stated that we could take their bodies to a crematorium down the road. All roads had them, because of the amount of death on every street. The workman wasn't messing with us when he said he wanted to work in the area. No time for funerals, no time for anything, just rebuild and forget about it.

I panicked. 'What do we do? We've no where to go!'

He cried in despair, 'Look, I don't care now. All my workers are dead, my home's destroyed, what can we do?'

'Rebuild, I guess,' I caved in, pointing at the workmen.

He faced the hard-hat men, shovelling out pits of once beautiful homes. Cedric's was one, mine was another. The size of Sydmouth was even more so. We took my parents and laid them in the crematorium the workman told us about. I said some prayers over them, and lit some candles, for Mother, Elli and Daddy, to remember them by.

I felt rather rotten at the whole thing, but those workmen had the right idea.

Rebuild they did, and rebuild we must.

CHAPTER XVII

Cedric and I were reeling from the deaths of family, friends, homes and whatever. And, we needed a break.

So, I asked again, 'What do we do?'

'Firstly, I want to go to a cash machine. See if our money's intact, or even the bank, for that matter. If not, we will starve,' Cedric suggested.

I carried on interrogating. 'What about that homeless shelter up the road?'

He huffed loudly. 'You listen to me,' he started to hold me at the arms. 'I will not even entertain THAT idea until we've exhausted our own resources, assuming we have any, and knowing my luck, maybe we can. I will gladly share them with you, if I must.'

That'll teach my impertinence to not have a big mouth.

'Anyway, we'll be alright. I've got friends, so if we need anything, I can call on them,' he added.

'Okay,' I muttered, walking beside another 'daddy'.

We went up to the bank, which was intact, but for some rubble at the front end. They hadn't cleared it away yet, so customers would walk over it to get to their money. Unfortunately, it was busy, too, so whoever was left surviving, would try to eliminate their accounts so they could put any relinquished funds in their mattresses. I thought that was a stupid and very archaic idea, but people have been known to do dumber things in other times.

The storefront next door was ravaged with bombing. The building after that was in the worst state possible.

No one survived either, but maybe for an old man or two, who were drinking out of bottles in bags, like the old days. This time, once they'd finished, they would trash their waste into the recycling pods laid out after the bombing. It was vital the factories were up and running and people throwing their waste into these pods, so we can destroy these aliens once and for all.

'I don't know if I could do this anymore,' I sounded still desperate.

'We've got to stick together if we're to survive. I'm sure we're clever enough to build back our lives, with new things and new ways to go about them.'

Cedric was such an optimist! Maybe I should think of it, but I can't because I've got Asperger's, and there is nothing I can do to stop myself from pooh-poohing any more possibilities.

'Yes, sir,' I droned on instead.

'My name's Cedric, remember? Do keep in step, you are not being walked on anymore.'

Oh jeez, I forgot. No, it was Lear who was manhandled, not me!! Yet, we both had the same condition, and one can contribute to another, despite the time shift, and differences between us. I had to think of something to get my head outta this mess. Elli, Daddy, ahhh. I wanted to suck my thumb in memory of such fantastic people. The ultimate security blankets. Cedric was nice enough, but ehh, he's too different. Maybe that was the point of people getting together. Differences were part of the swinging scenes of yore.

Now what did Elli and Daddy have in common, and myself for that matter? Ah yes, our Irish history, mingled in with other bits of Englishness, Italian, Germanic, ugh, what else was there??? I dwelled on the Irish, and tried to recall the great Muffyhuer and Cindihan.

Nah, they wouldn't have liked this place. I wondered if they'd dig me at all?

'Okay, Cindy, your turn,' Cedric called to me.

I woke up from my intense daydream, when I approached the stand at the bank.

I asked, 'What do I have?'

To which the teller asked, 'What do you want?'

Damn this fucking foible!

I hesitated, as I didn't want to take out all my money. 'Um...' I fumbled a bit, and Cedric noticed quickly.

'Excuse us,' Cedric took me aside. 'What the heck is wrong with you, do you want your money or don't you?'

I intensely looked at the wedding ring on my finger and Elli's ring on the opposite hand. I kept them there for safekeeping. 'What do I do with these?'

'What you want with them, I suppose,' he looked on ahead, gesturing the waiting people, to go forward.

This was going to take awhile.

'Look, I've got some money, and I'll help you, if that works out. We'll go to a pawnshop and we'll sell your rings,' Cedric suggested.

'Okay,' I began to walk out, before I began to cry again.

Other customers showed concern, but not surprised how such a young one like me could bear this shit. They thought Cedric was my father!

And 'daddy' stated to them, 'It's alright, just having a bad day. The girl will be alright.' To me, he ordered, 'Let's go.'

I walked out of the bank like a completely bombed out shell of a girl. I was just 20, as my last birthday was only last week. Cedric was still 'old' by many standards, but good enough to pal around with for comfort. I stared at the rings longingly, one ring knowing the union was between Mother and Elli; the other held the love between Elli and myself. I cried again.

'Cindy, get a hold of yourself. You're not the only one who's lost in this game. I've lost too, and imagine what those customers went through. Look, keep those rings. I know they will bring in something, but I saw you look at them, and I firmly believe you should have them. Keep the damn lot. They're more worthy on your fingers than it would be cash-in-hand. I think that would be a rather rotten way to remember your folks, eh? Besides, they look good on you.'

'Thanks,' I replied, after an hour-long pep talk. Okay, it wasn't an hour, but it FELT like forever!

I kept the rings on and went on our way toward a hotel. I was feeling rather hungry and told Cedric so.

'Okay, we'll get something to eat,' he said, 'Then we'll book into that hotel.'

We went past many houses, once beautiful houses, wrecked in the deluge. They were torn down, valuables removed and recycled toward the War effort. Building materials intact were saved and reused when they built new homes. If not, they'd go into a compactor and remade into something else. Something else sounded more appealing, I thought.

Unfortunately, my former home was also destroyed by the workmen, and rebuilt; so was Cedric's. I stayed with him; it seemed like a consolation prize on a game show of old. 'If you cannot get who you want, then check this fella out!' And so forth... I found we were dissimilar to live together, but we still made a good team. Our togetherness forged fond memories already.

I cried more to relieve myself, when Cedric desperately fought with the Asperger's. 'How do you think others feel now, huh? At least you've still got your mother's wedding band and that other ring! People have absolutely NOTHING! Even me. So, what I would do is stand up and walk proud among the living, because that is all that we have to do. Everybody else is rebuilding. What are you doing today?'

I wanted to pelt him one... nicely, but still pelt him one. Elli, Daddy, Mother! AUGGHH!! I missed them so much; why were they taken away??

We found a spot in a hotel, got a room, and finally, ate in their makeshift canteen.

The plush of the room did not serve well, and the cushions were removed. The endless faces of survivors were horrifying, and it made me think I was lucky I had Mother's and Elli's rings still and Cedric to rely upon. I guess I should have been thankful for Cedric's kindness, but it was difficult for me to show it. I think it would have been difficult to show forth on anybody.

CHAPTER XVIII

The next day, Cedric found some cash on his card and decided to go for a short hop away from Sydmouth.

He suggested, 'How about Brightpoole?'

'Sounds good,' I said, maybe the trip will take our minds off the War.

We went by train to Brightpoole. It was cosy, still, despite the era we lived in, but comfortable. I sat there doing nothing, and Cedric read a newspaper that was folded on the table.

I called out, 'Can I read the comics?'

'Sure honey,' he pulled out the 'funny papers' and gave them to me.

I read them, and the humour was enticing. Quite gritty, if you ask me, and soon, the shoreline of Brightpoole was evident. Pretty, yet unaffected by the War, it stayed in touch with the straggles of humanity that went there to escape, maybe live there.

'It says the aliens are asking for a truce; looks like the War is finally over.' Cedric read aloud, *'A statue was put up in Sydmouth Square in commemoration of Cynthia Lear, the base reading 'Remember Thine Own'.'*

'That's nice,' I bit my nails awhile as the shoreline's markings increased.

'It says here the aliens put surveillance materials in the statue,' he read on. 'Oh, it looks like we'd better watch out, eh?'

'Ha-ha, very funny,' I sassed him. 'Our stop is near.'

Cedric put the paper back, folded, on the table and left it there for someone else to read. Right now, we're on a vacation and no one or alien's going to destroy that!

We got off the train, had some lunch, then walked on the boardwalk, and some side roads. A pawn shop and antique place was back to back.

I looked at the wedding ring, and Elli's.

Cedric put his arm around me. 'Wanna pawn them now?'

I breathed outward and had to decide. Would they serve me now or later, or never?

I gulped, 'Let's go,' and headed for the pawn shop.

I showed the teller the rings, and he gave me a few hundred pounds for them.

'That'll keep you going,' he said.

'Much obliged,' I said, 'Is there a bank around here?'

'Just up the corner, there, y'can't miss it.'

'Thank you,' Cedric formally stated, rushing me out.

We went to the bank to cash in the lovely amount I got for the ring. I held a few pounds aside for personal use.

I remembered, 'Wait, can we visit that antique shop?'

'Sure, it's our vacation,' he said.

The antique shop was not far and I browsed through the window first. Among the many trinkets, photos, and some odd clothes, I saw something that intrigued me. It was a photo of someone with hair to his lower neckline, a small fringe, and mock-up medieval clothing.

I squealed, 'Who's that? He's a cutie!'

Cedric looked carefully at the photo.

'I think it's an actor by the name of DeMilo. It looks like it hails from an old Shakespeare production of Richard III, or something like that. I believe the fellow portrayed there is Hastings.'

'Oh,' I quietly uttered.

I thought about buying the photo, but decided not to. The price was fair, but there were more important things to think about at the moment, like where was I to live beyond the confines of the hotel? A new home, or flat, some food might be good too. I'd have to set up my place alone. Cedric looked as if he were in a faraway land somewhere, so I felt not to ask.

My job at the foundry allowed me some independence and freedom that comes with being young, despite the War. Now, that independence and freedom will come with a price; the price of living. The prospect of being on my own was more real than I liked, it frightened me. I took it to mean farewell to the only friend I'd known, save for my folks.

As if to read my mind, Cedric blurted out, 'You'll make new friends, I'm sure.'

I went completely off-topic, and walked away from the antique shop. 'I never lived on my own before.

'Well, you're going to do so now. It's about time, too. I'm inappropriate for your needs anyway,' he huffed. 'But, I have a friend who could help you.'

We ate lunch and decided to return to Sydmouth. It was a fair day, as best as you can get, and that weird creepy statue on the Square was now front and centre to all who passed it by. The thing looked exactly like me, I mean Lear, and it just stood there like a goliath. Eeewwhh, did it give me the creeps!

Cedric caught me looking at the statue and getting freaked out about it. 'Let me get your mind off that thing, Cindy. Let me tell you about Bellarouche.'

And so he did. Lacey Bellarouche. A dapper Frenchman (or someone who had the background, at least), he was younger than Cedric; still older than me. Good looking fellow, too, with a bit of grey at the sides. He might make the transition easier.

'He's also a good cook, so he can teach you a thing or two,' Cedric added.

Once we returned to Sydmouth, we returned to the hotel, and Cedric phoned up his friend. I was feeling the walls closing in on me, and found it hard to breathe. Not literally, of course, but in an 'orphaned' state, I felt myself in a bind, a spot tighter than normal. It seemed worse than it was, due to my condition.

I went frantic. 'What about my condition, what if he doesn't like me?'

Cedric had finished the call by now, and stood up to me, bowing his head. That was how short I was to him. 'Your condition, I said earlier, does not matter. What matters is your coping, and I think you will do marvellously.'

So I got told off, again, in a pleasant way.

He added, 'Besides, would I inform someone about you without telling them of your unseen problem?'

Guess that settled it.

I felt really bad, like I was a burden to everyone. Strangers, friends, family, all people. It made me very ashamed of myself.

'Lace will be around soon, so you might want to pack up,' Cedric said.

'Lace?'

'Yeah, it's his nickname. I've called him that for years. He used to work for me until he got into his bookish haunts and decided to work in a library. Maybe he can find a job for you?'

Guess that settled that one too.

I picked up whatever I had left. I went over to kiss Cedric.

'Thank you for what you've done for me. I hope I see you again sometime,' I exclaimed, giving him an additional hug.

'All in a day's work, my dear. I'm sorry you cannot work for me anymore. The foundry's had it, the War is over and I need time to rebuild. That's why I suggested Lace. He can help you get to where you need.'

What I needed was Daddy or Elli and a good stiff drink!

About an hour later, a knock was heard at the door; Cedric got up to greet his old friend. They spent some time together, as I finished packing.

'Lace,' Cedric cried, hugging him.

'Cedric, it is good to see you. You are looking, um, well,' Lace responded.

'Um, we'd been through a lot. Haven't we, Cindy?'

I nodded and got up to shake Lace's hand. It had a clammy, fleshy feel to it, as if something was underneath, but you couldn't pinpoint what it was. Probably a large callus or something. Probably moving books around.

'This is Cynthia Daye,' Cedric introduced me.

'Charmed. Absolutely lovely in dark times such as these,' he reached for my hand to kiss it.

It was a painful farewell for me and Cedric.

'We'll see each other again. You go with Lace, and rebuild yourself.'

I asked, 'What will you do?'

'Something, anything. I hadn't figured it out. I'm old though, not too old, but past the prime. You're just beginning. Go out there and show your stuff,' he encouraged.

He kissed me once last time, before opening the door to let Lacey and me out. It's been some time since I settled anywhere, and getting a new flat would be important. Still, I wondered about Lacey and how attractive he was. With dark eyes, greying hair, he was attractive in a fatalistic way. I couldn't put my finger on it; it was best not to. I thought I'd burn myself and that would put me in a bad place, especially as I had to rely on these people until I got myself straightened out.

We went outside and talked a bit. On the way, Lacey bought some food and such to take home and make.

Upon entering his place, he asked me if I wanted anything before dinner.

I answered, 'What've you got?'

'Well,' Lacey looked in the fridge, 'Juice, milk, soda...'

'Juice would be fine.'

He made up a glass for me and put it on the table.

'Cedric told me you may have interest in library work.'

'I guess. Do I have to go to school for that?'

'You would. I have a degree, so I can look into that for you.' He swigged his drink.

He took me into a spare room. The degree was on his wall.

'This is where you will sleep for the time being, until we settle an apartment for you somewhere.'

'Thanks. Could I stay in this block?'

'Perhaps. I can find out if there's one available. In the meantime, my place is yours.'

I smiled and hugged him. I helped him with dinner, from the stuff bought earlier.

'Frenchmen are good at cooking, even in the advanced state we live in now,' Lacey commented.

'And how,' I mulled over an omelette with vegetables.

He offered me a cookie from the tin, from a batch that he baked himself.

'Nice,' I mused, munching on a chocolate chip cookie.

I later helped him with the dishes, and got comfortable on the sofa. We watched television together. It felt weird to be with him, but nice. But it is tomorrow that will count and hopefully it will count for something.

CHAPTER XIX

Many years passed and I was now thirty-six, nearly thirty-seven. Things have come and gone for me and that War that we had was forever, a thing of the past. The problem was, so was my family, and if I forgot that fact, I wouldn't survive. Their love will always be with me; yet, I had to let go of them and move on to better pastures of life.

I worked in the library near Sydmouth Square, since meeting Lacey, where that creepy statue was. I was honoured that it was for my ancestor, Cynthia Lear, but the fire-weapon hand jive imposed on people who didn't respect it, I thought was too much. Likewise, I didn't have time to dwell on that, as Lacey's library connections proved useful to me. I went on a library course at night and got the degree. Yet, I still shelved books. It was a job, and at the time, I didn't care. I figured the degree could liven me up another time. Book shelving appealed to my condition immediately, and Lacey felt it was the best for me, for the moment.

And with this job came good dollops of money coming into view. I offered to help Lacey pay my way, and the collaboration helped greatly. He made a good roommate for me all these years, and there was nothing between us, but space between. He respected me like that, though I was a fully fledged woman now. If it had been Elli, I think I would be moving out pretty soon.

Cedric made the ragbags as an actor. The library had copies of them strewn about for all to see. He started doing Shakespeare productions, with a twist. The latest one was called 'Yo, Des!', which featured the entire play under the spell of old-school rap/hip-hop. That would be most interesting to watch with someone you like, or loved, but alas, I had nobody. It would also help if you were a fan of the musical genre, too, and not just Shakespeare. He was a very old-school, old-world fellow. I wondered what he would have been like as a person nowadays, as opposed to judging him via his many performances.

Meanwhile, Lacey had been seeing another woman recently. There were others, I was certain, but this one was more focused on his mind. But, Lacey and I were friends, nothing more. I didn't expect that treatment from him. He was more fatherly to me than anything. A twenty year age gap would do that sort of thing.

He announced the illustrious event during our evening meal after work. My heart stopped beating for a second.

I sounded surprised, 'Another girl?'

'A fantastic girl. Kind of like you, but more my age. You're a little young for me, yet.'

Me young? I didn't think so. 'Can I meet her?'

'Sure, you can. We've been seeing one another for some time.'

Me and my big mouth! All I could utter was 'Uhhh.'

'Don't worry, child. I understand your frustration. You really wanted me, didn't you, eh? Like Cedric of the old days?'

Why put Cedric into this now????

He continued, 'All this time we've worked and fussed together, but we never took the time to, you know, go forth.'

I wondered, Go forth into WHAT????

I sighed and wondered what Cedric was up to. By now, he'd have been sixty or something. Good God, I'm surrounded by human ageing!

'It's okay,' I reconciled. 'I wasn't keen on you anyway.'

There, it was plainly stated! I cried then.

'There, there,' Lacey sounded like a mother hen. 'Come here.' He gave me a hug. 'Better?'

NO IT WASN'T!

'Yeah, I guess,' I lied. 'I'm too little, then.'

'My dear, you're just a fraction too little for me,' he said, measuring the minute amount with his thumb and forefinger. 'You just hadn't met the right one.'

YES I DID, YOU DUMBFUCK!

And it was Elli, but I wouldn't tell him that. I stuck to my guns, however big they were. I wanted to blast sense into the wall behind his head, and he got trapped between. Yet, walls didn't yield sometimes...

... and neither did he. 'Stop looking at me like that,' he cried. 'Wash up, girl, she'll be here soon.'

I got up, 'What?'

'Yes, I invited her here, then we'll go to dinner and a show. Your man, Cedric's in another one of his goofy productions. I think it's called 'Yo, Des!' It's an Othello remake or something.'

Why did grownups have all the fun. Hey, wait a minute, I'M A GROWNUP TOO!

I asked sardonically, 'What's her name then?'

'Carion Arquet.'

'Sounds lost to me,' I uttered to myself.

A while later, a knock came to the door. Lacey opened it.

'Lacey Bellarouche,' the answer came, as the speaker threw herself upon the gentleman.

'Come in come in, welcome,' Lacey closed the door. 'Let me look at you.' He perused her quickly, as he was a quick reader, even in life. 'You look lovely and delicious.'

Brown eyes, brown/blackish hair, cream coloured dress and accompanying heels. Perfect date for a lost container like Lacey, or a powerful artefact therein.

Lacey ordered me, 'Cynthia, come here.'

I walked up to him, and he put his arm around me. 'Carion, this is Cynthia, my little friend at the library.'

'Ohh,' Carion squealed, 'You're one of the many pages who book shelve, aren't you?'

What an introduction!

'I am. Where I'm needed,' I intoned greatly, or as great as possible. 'Done so for many years.'

'Good gosh,' she cried. 'Must be boring for you now. Haven't you a degree?'

'Got one, but still stay at the bottom for now.'

'She's happy,' Lacey commented dismissively, 'How about dinner, and that show you wanted?'

'Oh, yes, please,' Carion cooed. 'Nice to meet you Cynthia.'

'Likewise,' I droned on.

He got his coat, and glanced at me, 'You're free to do what you want. Keep the fort intact for me, eh?'

'Yes, sir,' I added.

'And we'll have no more of that 'yes sir'; my name is Lacey. Remember that.'

I stared in silence as the lovebirds twitched out the door. I hoped their time goes okay, but the play may be the end of them. I read that Cedric was very cutting in his work; possibly being the best in the acting world. I sighed, and turned the television on, hoping for something to watch to take the mind off this madness. I found being the equivalent to 'kid sister' rather annoying and an absolute menace, mostly of a ghostly sort, because I hid those feelings from Lacey.

Making friends wasn't that easy for me. I had a cat named Brian, but he died recently. I was very distraught about it, but at least he had a long run in life. I hoped I prove that lucky. The emptiness raged in my heart, similar to what I went through in losing Elli. Mother was one huge loss, but Elli, and what he represented to me, was too much. There was nothing to do but mourn.

The show on the monitor was about a mid-Western town that gets visited by someone of another century. Sounded good, and better than moping around, thinking of someone else's fun instead of my own. Problem was, all I got was nothing. My job was freakish, and I've been living with someone who may flee into a romantic dream on the steps of antiquity. Everybody felt older than me. I was not young, either, but I certainly did not feel old. Maybe I would make a good catch for someone.

I didn't know, and didn't care. The show was interesting at least, but it would have been nice if things happened to me. At least one of the characters looked like Daddy and Elli, so that was a huge comfort. I wandered around in my mind, looking for blame, and found none. If it was Lear, well, everyone would be a target, and they were, cos we fought a huge War over it.

When the show was over, I switched off and went to bed. I wasn't comfortable, staying up for someone with a link or whatever in his arms.

Next morning, I woke up to find my roommate buzzing with excitement.

He asked excitedly, 'Have you heard?'

Without looking up, I returned, 'No. What?'

He sat down, holding my hand. 'I've proposed to her.'

'Miss Arquet?'

'Miss Arquet.'

'Good for you. I hope she opens up to you. Don't get your face blown away, now.'

'She will, with a bit of encouragement. My face is indestructible.'

He smiled and kept on with breakfast. I was hungry, I usually am. I let him lavish his skills upon me. If this guy was getting married, then where would I be if I didn't have cooking skills?

'Aren't you going to congratulate me?'

I looked at him. 'Thought I did. Suits you.'

'Yes, she does,' he fiddled with his necktie. 'Jealous?'

I didn't want to say it but, YES!

'Well, we come by situations like these in leaps and bounds. Your leap and bound may lie elsewhere, I reckon,' he said.

I started to cry. Bitterly. My family, for myself, maybe for Carion and Lacey.

He gave me a hug. 'Your time will come, don't worry. This must have been a shock to you.'

Worse than a shock, I thought, a lost cause: mine!

'Your time will come,' he continued to comfort me.

'When's the date?'

'A few weeks. I'm packing up to go abroad. Long term. There are libraries and things there I want to explore and I'm in the running for a job out there.'

Big deal, my mind echoed. You get everything. Everyone gets everything, and I don't!

'I've booked you for another library conference,' he carried on, 'At the Hotel Klaaxon. You'll love it, and you never know.'

Great, get a date at a dork convention. What was he thinking?!

'And, you can take over the rent on this flat. You've got a home for as long as you need. Carion and I will find something abroad.'

'Thank you,' I tried to sound grateful, but...

'Gives you a good place to live, no?'

I went up to Lacey and hugged and kissed him. Maybe I could pretend he was Elli?? Nah, he was giving me the flat, not his life.

'Carion's department is going too,' he added. 'Mostly for underlings. You'll benefit. You know how it is.'

Sure I will; big deal, I repeated! He gets the girl; I go to a library convention. Whoopee! I felt like a guest at a park full of dinosaurs.

'Yes,' I whispered.

'Don't be like that. You know it's for the best. You can be Carion's maid of honour, or one of them.'

'Why would she want me?'

'I insisted,' he grinned. 'I figured it'll do you some good. I know about your condition. Cedric told me about it long ago. I know it doesn't go away and that you have to live with it all your life.'

'Doesn't the bride choose?'

'Well,' he smiled, 'In this case, I chose for her.'

He gave me a kiss for reassurance and went off somewhere, probably to the toilet in the direction he was heading.

* * * * * *

The wedding was a success for Carion and Lacey. We went to a local registry office, instead of a church, as they were irreligious. They didn't want lost archs or flying angels raining on their parade.

As promised, Lacey gave me the keys to the flat before he left. He was correct in wanting to live abroad, and he went off with Carion to that faraway land of... wherever. I never heard from him again and I'd wondered what happened to him. Did he ever find the golden doll of his dreams in Carion?

My place in that Klaaxon conference was secured, and it was coming up in a few days or so.

Lacey thought it would be better for my career in library work. I'd go somewhere with it, and stop book shelving, finally. The many years I did it, it didn't get beyond where I was. It made good money, and I enjoyed it. There was a glut in the market, and for someone who has a degree, I found it pathetic that I carried on shelving books.

Yet, I accepted it, and let it ride. There was nothing for me at the present moment. No more family, and the few friends I did have, went separate ways to me. It was always like that. There was no choice between death and a part of the pathways. Friends were difficult to come by, and even more so to come back to. I was damn lucky to be doing this job in the first place...

... and I reckoned I had an interesting future to face.